Collector's Edition

Time
Not Measured
By A Clock

Cowboy Poetry
by Carole Jarvis

From the life of a cowboy's wife

Illustrated by Larry Bute

Cowboy Miner PRODUCTIONS

Time Not Measured by a Clock, Cowboy Poetry by Carole Jarvis, From the life of a cowboy's wife
Copyright © 2003 Carole Jarvis
Illustrations copyright © 2003 Carole Jarvis

Publisher:
  Cowboy Miner Productions
  P.O. Box 9674
  Phoenix, AZ 85068
  Phone: (602) 596-6063
  www.CowboyMiner.com
All rights reserved.
Band-Aid® is a registered trademark of Johnson & Johnson.

Publisher's Cataloging-in-Publication Data
Jarvis, Carole, 1935—
Time Not Measured by a Clock : Cowboy Poetry by Carole Jarvis, From the life of a cowboy's wife / Carole Jarvis.
    p. cm. Illustrated.
    ISBN: 1-931725-07-1
1. Cowboy Poetry—Arizona. 2. Ranch Life—Arizona.
3. Western History (U.S.)—Poetry. 4. Poetry—Arizona
Historical. 5. Women—Ranch Life.
    I. Title
Library of Congress Control Number: 2003108984

Design & Typesetting: SageBrush Publications, Tempe, Arizona
Cover Design: SageBrush Publications
Front Cover Photo: Sharron Tarter
    Dan Jarvis on Stretch with his dog Jake.
Back Cover Photo: Shell Beck
Printing: Bang Printing, Brainerd, Minnesota

Printed and bound in the United States of America

Contents

Foreword

Selecting poetry was never one of my favorite jobs in my years at *Western Horseman* magazine. Part of that was because you had to tell so many people something they didn't want to hear. A few of those people helpfully told me that I really didn't know much about poetry.

They were right. I don't pretend to be an expert, but I did know what the readers expected to see in the magazine. That's why I was always happy to receive an envelope from Carole Jarvis. From the first one she sent us, her poetry fit us like a warm coat on a cold morning. In fact, I had to send some poems back to Carole because I still had several in the drawer that had not yet been printed and felt guilty about it.

The best poetry puts feelings into a package that, when opened and read, delivers those feelings intact. In addition to the poems used in the magazine, we picked several by Carole to be used on our Cowboy Calendar.

I was pleased to learn that Larry Bute was doing the illustrations for this book, and even more pleased when I saw them. Larry and Carole each convey their devotion to ranching, the West, and the way of life that so many of us envy.

This book opens a window to a world some of you may never be able to visit any other way. For others, it provides a look back to a place forsaken but not forgotten. These poems paint mental pictures and create emotional music. Thank you, Carole, for this gift.

Gary Vorhes
Retired editor-in-chief
Western Horseman magazine

5

Dan Jarvis, 1957, Wickenburg, Arizona

Introduction

This book is dedicated to all the cowboys and ranchers and their wives, who are the unsung heroes of the West today. The obstacles they have always had to overcome—drought, predators, disease—pale in comparison to the battles they now fight to maintain their way of life. They now face NAFTA, the Endangered Species Act, and environmental groups that are helped by elected members of our own government, whose sole objective is to remove cattle and ranching from the West. May God give them the strength they need in these battles.

For years I've wanted to put some of my poems and stories about my life with, and around cowboys, into a book, and I talked about it, but that's as far as it went.

At the Cowboy Poetry Gatherings, I was often asked, "Do you have a book?" My answer routinely would be, "Well, not yet, but it's in my plans." It actually got to be embarrassing ducking the answer to the question, "When is your book coming out?"

Then came Lee Raine into my acquaintance and friendship. She is a writer, photographer, and marvel at anything to do with computers. Through her, I had the opportunity to personally meet Gary Vorhes, who was for many years Managing Editor for *Western Horseman* magazine, and who is one of those responsible for accepting some of my poems for publication in the magazine over the years.

Gary graciously offered to edit this book for me, and Lee put all the material on her computer and got it ready to go to the publisher. So, if it was not for these two I would, no doubt, still be ducking the same question! *Muchas gracias, amigos!*

And, needless to say, having Larry Bute do the illustrations for my book has been "the icing on the cake." My thanks to him for his excellent illustrations that reflect the feel and style of my poems and stories.

I grew up in Southern California, on the edge of Anaheim, a relatively small town back then, but that has since earned a place on the map as the home of Disneyland. The orange groves and fields that I rode horseback through, are long gone and have been replaced with Tomorrowland, Fantasyland, and Frontierland.

Carole in her teens.

My first experience with horses came at the age of three at a little ranch out in the Mojave Desert in California. My folks had friends who, even back then, worked off of the ranch at a paying job so they could support their "ranching habit." A little gentle mustang mare, not more than 13 hands, had raised the owner's kids, and began my love affair with horses.

Carole on the first horse she ever rode. With her are her mother, father and brother.

As I grew up, horses were always a part of my life, but I didn't actually own one until I finished school and went to Arizona to work. I bought a two-year old colt because I wanted to "break my own horse." As I remember, we both got a whole lot of learning that first year! But he did turn out to be a great little using horse.

The second fascination in my life was cowboys. Like so many of my generation, I grew up in the era of Saturday matinee westerns and for those few hours in the darkness of the theatre, I could be the heroine and the one who lived happily ever after with the noble, handsome cowboy, and his beautiful golden palomino (in the case of my favorite, Roy Rogers).

As this same young girl, I dreamed of a ranch, a cowboy, and a horse. Actually, lots of horses. But unlike many other girls who outgrew these dreams, I never did. So it was natural I would gravitate to places where there was ranching and cowboys when I "grew up." One such place was Jackson Hole, Wyoming. My second summer working there, I met a handsome cowboy who actually came riding by the cabin where I was living, on a gorgeous coal-black filly. I've been teased about whether I was smitten by the filly or the cowboy first! Well, whichever it was, the cowboy is the one that's still around, and in 2003, we celebrated our forty-fifth wedding anniversary.

We've lived and cowboyed in Wyoming, Oregon and Arizona. There's been a lot of hard work, dusty trails, blisters, sunburns and broken bones along the way, but it's the life I chose and the one my husband Dan chose. We wouldn't trade it for any other.

As one of my poems begins, "There's a whole lot of satisfaction in the way a cowboy lives, not the hard work and the danger, but the freedom that it gives." And it ends with this verse, "When his long days' over, and his pony's turned out to graze, he's filled with satisfaction from the job, not what it pays. And he'll walk through the door of his old bunk house, with his dog just one step behind, content with his life as a cowboy, and the peace it brings to his mind." I guess that says it all.

Photo by Sharron Tarter

Dan and Carole—Oregon Ranch Country

"They're up and out before dawn lights the sky"

I'm Glad I Still Live Where There's Cowboys

I'm glad I still live where there's cowboys
    who earn a wage makin' a hand.
Like their counterparts from another time,
    these cowboys still ride for a brand.

When a group of 'em gather for roundup,
    it's like turnin' back a page
In a book on the history of cowboys,
    from a different time and age.

They're up and out before dawn lights the sky,
    some youngsters, some old buckaroos.
Each share a kinship for this way of life,
    and each one has paid his dues.

I love watchin' 'em bring the cows in,
    calves trailin' along beside.
And I'm thinkin', it won't be long now,
    'til those calves wear a brand on their hide.

I like listenin' to their quiet western drawls,
    watchin' as they ride with such ease,
Jinglin' spurs hung on scuffed high-heel boots,
    and a good horse between their knees.

Cowboys in Levi or Wrangler jeans,
    wearin' denim shirts with snaps,
Those dusty, sweatstained, old black Stetsons,
    and tight-fittin' leather chaps.

These same men are partial to pickups—
    primarily, the four-wheel-drive kind,
Which they load with hay bales and cowdogs,
    then pull a stock trailer behind.

You can hear their rigs comin' for miles,
    and see the dust in the air.
They drive like they're out chasin' rustlers,
    'stead of only goin' somewhere!

Maybe haulin' a cow to the vet,
    or a load of calves to a sale,
Bringin' back fencin' supplies from town,
    or just pickin' up the mail.

There's always work to be done on a ranch,
    and I seldom hear cowboys balk.
One exception to the rule, of course—
    if the job means havin' to walk!

Yes, I'm glad I still live where there's cowboys,
    'cause they're men on good terms with life.
And in them, the spirit of the West still lives;
    I should know, I'm a cowboy's wife.

Once A Cowboy, Always A Cowboy

See that cowboy there? He used to ride the roughstring—
    they say he was as good as they came.
If someone had a bad one, couldn't be ridden,
    when he got done that cayuse would be tame.

They never bucked too hard or reared too high,
    he'd sit there like he didn't give a damn,
But when he finally got their 'full attention',
    that bronc was meek and mild as any lamb.

That was in his twenties and his thirties,
    the two decades when cowboys hit their stride.
By his forties and his fifties he'd slowed up some,
    but he still could give those ponies a good ride.

Then old broken bones and fractures, dislocations,
    that never bothered him when he was young,
Came back to haunt him on a daily basis,
    and he recalled the wrecks for every one!

Now past sixty, he's still a ridin' green ones,
    and still turns out a darn good usin' horse.
With his gimmicks and his hundred ways to cheat 'em,
    he doesn't have to use as much brute force!

'Cause it's a fact of life, as he grows older,
    he'll have to use more brain and less of brawn,
Since there'll always be a horse that needs some ridin',
    and that cowboy, if he's able, will get on!

"Lightnin' just struck the top of a pine!"

All's Well That Ends Well

A Day In The Life Of A Mom And Pop Cow Operation

(The cowboy speaks:)

Hey Honey, gotta move those cows today,
    from down here to the pasture on top.
Shouldn't take more than a couple of hours,
    it's only a skip and a hop.

(The cowboy's wife answers:)

Oh? Okay, I'd planned to do washing,
    but guess it can wait one more day.
Besides, the radio said chance of showers,
    and a storm might be headed this way.

Naw, there's not a sign of a cloud,
    in any direction out there,
And we'll be back long before lunch,
    with plenty of time to spare.

Then why do I have these misgivings,
    that keep flitting through my brain?
That woman's intuition thing,
    it's somethin' that's hard to explain.

Stop worryin'! I'll catch the horses,
    saddle up, and we'll get on our way.
We gotta check all the fence as we go,
    and maybe we'll spot that old stray.

I'll put some beans in the crock-pot,
  get my hat and coat and be there.
If you'd told me last night we were goin',
  I'd have had more time to prepare!

It happens, I didn't know last night,
  just rode out this mornin' to check.
The grass is getting' short down here,
  and they don't gain on short grass, by heck!

He's out the door and I scramble,
  put the pinto beans on to cook,
Grab two apples, one sack of peanuts,
  and my old work coat off the hook.

What took you so long? I'm all saddled,
  and your mare is ready to go.
Bring those cows down out of the corner,
  I'll bring them up from below.

We're on our way and it's not quite eight.
  I see the pasture gates are set.
If things go smooth, there's still a chance
  we might be home by noon yet!

Don't let 'em lag, keep 'em stringin' out,
  and push in those three on your right!
I see a hole in the fence over there,
  I'll go stretch those wires up tight.

This grass we're crossing is good,
    and the cows don't want to move on.
I wish he'd hurry up and get back,
    I swear it's an hour he's been gone!

I can't believe those old fence posts,
    rotted right off at the ground!
Who'd of thought that stretchin' one wire
    would bring the whole dang fence down?

Oh great! I've got cows behind me,
    and there goes some off to the side!
I can't keep 'em bunched in *or* movin',
    no matter how hard I ride!

Well, my five-minute job took forty,
    bet Carole's clear up to the gate.
Movin' those critters alone can be tough,
    if those cows don't cooperate!

Get up there you four-footed Big Mac!
    Boy, could I use a dog now!
But *he's* watchin' Dan stretch bob wire,
    while *I'm* out here chasin' the cow!

Uh oh, I can see we've got trouble!
    those cattle have scattered out wide.
Here comes Carole, hell bent for leather,
    and she's lookin' a little wall-eyed!

What happened?! No, I don't want to hear—
 it's only five miles to the top,
But counting all my trips back and forth,
 comes to more than your "skip and a hop"!

Sorry! It was one of those things;
 I'll explain when we get the cows back.
Right now just keep this bunch movin',
 and don't give 'em any slack!

Another simple half-a-day's job,
 I ought to know better by now!
There's no such thing as a schedule,
 if it *ever* involves a cow!

Okay, I've got 'em all back now,
 and the front ones are linin' out nice.
Look at the good side, its summer,
 we're not ridin' in snow and ice!

That makes me feel *so* much better—
 here, have an apple for lunch!
And lookin' up at those black clouds,
 we'd better start shovin' this bunch!

You're right, the weather is changin',
 come on, the gate's just up there.
You push 'em thru, I'll count 'em,
 and we don't have much time to spare!

Swell! Now there's lightnin' and thunder—
    we'll be lucky if they don't break and run!
And here comes the rain—great big drops—
    we'll be soaked before we get done!

Get that gate shut; I got a good count,
    they're all in, lets head off this hill!
If you don't want to get wet to the hide,
    you'd better show your ridin' skill!

It's too late for hurryin' to help,
    the rain's pourin' off my hat brim!
Lightnin' just struck the top of a pine,
    right behind us up on that rim!

For gosh sakes, motivate that mare!
    Bein' on a horse in a storm,
Is just temptin' the fates with lightnin',
    so make that old girl perform!

You ride your horse, and I'll ride mine,
    and we'll see who's the first to get back!
I don't need a guide to show me the way,
    and I don't need to follow a track!

Well, there she goes, come on old horse,
    it kinda looks like she's mad.
Gettin' wet and a few hours late,
    that sure ain't the worst day we've had!

We're back, old girl—off comes the saddle,
 and you could use some oats, I bet.
.There hangs my slicker, right in the tack room;
 well, at least *it* didn't get wet!

You beat me, but I had to close gates.
 I'll unsaddle, give Baldy his grain.
You go get dry and dish up those beans!
 Boy, this shore is a good rain!

The house is warm, and my mood has improved,
 with the thought of those beans and dry clothes.
Yeah, we had a few setbacks, but got the job done,
 and that's just the way cowboyin' goes!

A Guest Of Mother Nature

I watched the moon play hide and seek
   with the clouds tonight,
      as the lightning in the distance lit the sky.
The wind that comes before a storm
   carried the scent of rain,
      but it looked like it was all going to pass us by.

From somewhere on the desert
   came a coyote's serenade,
      then the distant thunder's rumble veiled the sound,
As I sat there on my front porch,
   easing down my mind,
      like when something that you'd lost has just been found.

The wind, blowing through the pine,
   was almost like a whisper,
      contrasting with a raucous, croaking toad.
Then the splat, splat staccato
   of raindrops on the roof,
      began to clatter, like a message sent in code.

Capricious Mother Nature
   sometimes gives, sometimes takes;
      it's impossible to calculate her whim.
Like a cleric with a mission,
   all the world is her church,
      and the wind, and rain, and thunder are her hymn.

Her Little Boy

You can tell where he's been
    by the tracks across the floor,
Comin' in from the back porch
    then out the front door.

With a stop in the kitchen
    for a mid-morning snack.
Homemade bread and some jelly,
    (which is never put back!)

A peanut butter jar,
    but the lid's not around.
Just a knife stickin' in it
    like a post in the ground.

How often she's asked him,
    "Honey, please wipe your feet.
And put the lid back on food,
    after you eat.

"Use that soap on your hands,
    don't just wet 'em and wipe.
The towel when you're done
    is a gross-awful sight!"

Then those little-boy eyes,
    like a big Irish Setter,
Cast a half-guilty look—
    yeah, he'll try to do better.

He gives her a hug,
    and a peck on the cheek,
But she swears that he's deaf
    to her frequent critique!

His mind's on his playthings—
    tractors, trucks and his horse.
Which leaves darn little time,
    to feel much remorse.

Besides, she remembers,
    as she puts things away,
He's been just like he is,
    since their wedding day.

"You can tell where he's been by the tracks across the floor"

"I watch my old friend restin' by a tree"

Catch

Well, I finally put the old horse out to pasture;
   he's lame now, and can't travel like he should.
But he gave sixteen honest years to this cow outfit,
   and would give another sixteen if he could.

His mama dropped him early one September,
   on a mornin' when the ground was white with frost.
And it didn't take much time 'til we all figured,
   he was worth a whole lot more than what he'd cost.

We'd bought the mare that spring at some darn auction,
   a three-year-old, unbroke, but smooth and nice.
We didn't know she had a foal inside her,
   or to tell the truth, we'd never have looked twice.

But although we didn't know about his daddy,
   I'll tell you what, he had to be *some* stud,
'Cause that little colt turned into somethin' special,
   the kind you only get from real good blood.

There never was a doubt as what to name him,
   from the day that he was born we called him Catch,
And by the time his bridle teeth were comin' in,
   as a cowboy's horse, he didn't have a match.

No calf was born that ever could outrun him,
    and you'd better have your loop spun out my friend,
'Cause Ol' Catch would put you just where you should be,
    right up on that little calf's rear end!

Cuttin' cattle out, when a herd was all mixed up,
    I'd swear he knew a steer from some old cow.
I'd just point him toward the critter I was after,
    and he always knew which one, don't ask me how.

You'll hear a cowboy say a horse has "bottom",
    which really means he's tough, with lots of go.
And I never rode a horse that was his equal,
    when he was in his prime, some years ago.

Before the dawn would even break the skyline,
    we'd be headed up some draw to hunt for strays.
Sometimes gettin' back just as the sun set;
    if you covered half that ranch you'd rode a ways!

There were times a bog would have an old cow captured,
    with no chance she'd ever get loose on her own.
Mired up to her belly in the gumbo,
    nothin' 'round her, trapped there all alone.

Pathetic-lookin', worn down with her struggles,
    I'd rope her horns to pull her on dry land.
Her a-hookin' and a-fightin' at the rescue,
    too dumb to know salvation was at hand.

But Catch could outmaneuver her plumb easy;
    I'd flip my rope around her muddy hip,
Give a jerk before she got her wind back,
    and have her on the ground, with one good trip.

That's when ol' Catch and me, we made a team!
    I'd jump off fast, to get my rope turned loose.
He'd hold that twine stretched tight, 'til I got there,
    then give me slack, so's I could slip my noose.

Oh, we had our share of wrecks from time to time—
    a cowboy just can't keep from takin' spills.
But I know there was a bunch of them I missed,
    thanks to Catch's savvy and his skills.

Now, lookin' back, I just can't keep from wonderin',
    as I watch my old friend restin' by a tree,
If I'll ever have a cowhorse half as honest,
    as that unexpected "catch colt's"* been to me.

---

*   A term used when a mare unexpectedly turns up in
    foal. Usually, the mare has been in a pasture with a
    young stallion that the owner hadn't thought was old
    enough to be a "dad."

"It's been almost a year now"

His Only Son

Western Horseman Magazine first published this poem in 1969 during the Viet Nam War.

It's been almost a year now,
  since Charlie went away,
a fact that Daddy never shows,
  yet he counts each and every day,

For Charlie was his only son,
  and though he loved all three,
a part of him was in that boy
  that eluded Sis and me.

Ranch folks have a closer bond
  than any other kind,
and from the day that boy could walk,
  he was never hard to find.

Wherever Dad went he would go,
  no matter what the season,
to help fix fence or set a post,
  he didn't need a reason.

How proud Dad was the first time
  that Charlie roped a calf,
but then fell off when old Buck stopped—
  we tried hard not to laugh.

But he kept growing, Charlie did,
  and kept on learning too,
'til there was nothing on the ranch
  that Charlie couldn't do.

They mowed the hay in summertime
  and stacked it in a row,
fed it out in winter's months
  when icy winds would blow.

Then in the big ranch kitchen
  when supper was all through,
Dad and Charlie talked about
  the many things they'd do.

The bull calf that they *knew* would top
  next spring's yearling sale,
the well pump that they ordered,
  it came clear out by rail.

They both would roll a cigarette
  and then my dad would say,
"Guess we'd better get some rest,
  tomorrow's another day."

But one tomorrow brought the word
  that Charlie had to go
and fight a war to keep the peace,
  just how we didn't know.

So Charlie kissed us girls goodbye,
  and shook his daddy's hand,
and soon the letters that he wrote
  were sent from a foreign land.

He vaguely spoke of missions,
    and battles that they fought,
but most of all he wrote about
    the things he missed a lot.

Mom's homemade bread and apple pies,
    cold milk, and fresh churned butter,
a windmill softly creaking,
    the kittens with their mother.

Pain would fill my daddy's eyes,
    as the letter was put away,
he'd take my mother's hand in his;
    they'd bow their heads to pray.

And Sis and I, well, we'd pray too,
    and ask the Lord above,
to bring our Charlie safely back,
    and guard him with His love.

And then we'd add another prayer,
    "Oh please God, let wars end,
so everyone can live in peace
    the way that You intend.

And all the Charlies can come home
    to those who wait and pray,
and fill the empty lives they left
    the day they went away."

"The littlest cowboy had brought Christmas home"

The Littlest Cowboy

Christmas was comin' at the old Rafter L,
   little less than one week away,
And us three cowboys who rode for that brand,
   were discussin' what we'd do that day.

None of us waddies was married at the time,
   and we had no families nearby,
So we guessed we'd spend Christmas on the ranch,
   maybe Cookie would bake us a pie.

Just about then, came a knock on the door,
   and the boss of the outfit walked in.
He said he was needin' a favor from us,
   some help for one of his kin.

So Mickey says, "What are you needin', Boss?
   We'll sure help ya' out if we can."
This ramrod had always been square with us,
   and we tried to do right by the man.

"I got a little nephew, boys," he tells us,
   "gonna spend the holidays here.
He's crazy about cowboys and horses,
   turned eight on his birthday this year."

"If you boys could spare, say an hour, on Christmas,
    and bring old Red up from pasture,
Maybe let Todd take a real short ride;
    but just in a walk, nothin' faster."

"Ya' see, the boy just finished with chemo,
    and a pretty long hospital stay,
And I got to thinkin' it might help him out
    to play cowboy, if just for a day."

We looked at each other, then nodded to him,
    he could count on the help of all three.
Then Mickey and me, we went into town,
    and Johnnie went after a tree.

Well, the next few days we spent our spare time
    puttin' up decorations we'd bought,
And trimmin' the piñon that Johnnie had found,
    the purtiest one ever, we thought.

By Christmas mornin' the lights were all strung,
    and three presents lay under the tree.
A small pair of boots, a hat, and some spurs,
    from Mickey, and Johnnie and me.

Old Red stood saddled, and his sorrel hide gleamed;
    he'd never been brushed that darn hard!
And we were decked out in our best cowboy gear,
    when the family drove into the yard.

There was huggin' and handshakes all around,
    then the boss brought Todd over to meet us.
I couldn't help notice, the frail little hand,
    he eagerly stuck out to greet us.

But his brown eyes were bright with excitement,
    and he had a grin as wide as the sky.
And seein' his face, when we gave him his presents,
    made a memory no money could buy.

His cowboy hat was a little too big,
    so we made an adjustment there.
Some folded newspaper took up the slack—
    we'd forgotten that Todd had no hair.

He pulled on his boots, we strapped on the spurs,
    and took him to meet old Red,
Then boosted him up into the saddle;
    "Can I ride by myself?" he said.

"You bet, Buckaroo!" Johnnie exclaimed,
    "Here's the reins, I'll just walk alongside."
In all my born days I've sure never seen,
    a face that showed any more pride!

As we watched, Todd happily circled old Red,
    and I knew we would all agree,
The littlest cowboy had brought Christmas home,
    for Mickey and Johnnie and me.

"*He rode for outfits everywhere*"

Connection

He was his daddy's shadow
   from the time that he could walk,
And "horse" and "cow" his favorite words
   when he first learned to talk.

He could coil a rope and throw it
   by the time that he was three,
And no one ever doubted
   what he'd grow up to be.

But his mama was the one
   who tucked him into bed,
Patched up his scrapes and bruises,
   and made sure his prayers were said.

While his daddy taught him ranchin',
   how to ride and swing a rope,
His mama taught compassion,
   and faith, and love, and hope.

He grew into youthful manhood
   wearin' cowboy boots and jeans.
Had the makin' of a top hand,
   by the time he'd reached his teens.

Then dreamin' a cowboy's dream,
   he headed out on his own,
While his mama kept on prayin',
   like before her boy was grown.

He rode for outfits everywhere
    and tried to stay in touch,
But a cowboy workin' for a brand
    just don't get free that much.

Sometimes days and weeks on end
    no human face he'd see,
Just his horse and Border collie,
    to keep him company.

Yet always deep inside him,
    he never felt alone.
Something out there, somewhere,
    connected him to home.

The times when he had troubles,
    and he'd like to walk away,
He'd remember things his mama said,
    and how she'd always pray,

And tell him there was nothin'
    that couldn't be resolved
With grit and perseverance,
    if he kept the Lord involved.

So he'd bow his head with simple faith,
    like he'd been taught to do,
Knowing every prayer he prayed,
    was multiplied by two.

The Reluctant Cowboy Carpenter

He rebuilds a stretch of old fence, good as new,
  and at hangin' gates, knows just what to do.
He builds corrals from scratch, does all their repair.
  He'll climb a windmill tower, and work way up there.

I see new saddle racks, so the tack room's all done.
  Reinforcing on the loading chute's just begun.
With chainsaw and hammer, the ranch he'll maintain,
  except for the house, which he calls MY domain!

The porch roof is sagging, my ceiling fan quit,
  two windows won't open, and the door screen is split.
A bath faucet drip, sometimes keeps me awake,
  then the drain plugs up! Gotta find me that "snake"!

The kitchen floor gives, each time I cross it.
  The couch is worn out, I'd sure like to toss it,
But the money for that, just bought a tire,
  ten bags of cement, and six rolls of barb wire!

Now Fall has arrived, and he's back in the saddle,
  ridin' each day to gather the cattle.
So his carpenter projects have been put on hold,
  which suits him just fine, if the truth be told.

Well, I saw a two-by-four, out in the woodpile,
  I'll prop that porch roof; prob'ly do for a while.
And find some washers, try and stop that dang drip,
  duct tape the screen, and patch up the rip.

I don't need the fan—Autumn is here,
  so those windows can stay shut, least 'til next year.
Maybe *then* that cowboy will do MY repair.
  Who am I kidding?—I don't have a prayer!

"When three or four sound like a dozen strong"

Coyote

They've woke me in the mornin',
   and the middle of the night,
And I sometimes just lay listenin' to their song.

There's a little hint of lonely,
   in that coyote serenade,
When three or four sound like a dozen strong.

But then, maybe all that yappin',
   and howlin' at the moon,
Is nothin' more than quartet harmony,

From a bunch of gray-brown coyotes,
   merely tryin' to get by,
Not so different from the likes of you and me.

Don't ya' s'pose his heart goes dancin',
   in the springtime of the year,
When a rain shower makes the air so fresh and clean?

Kinda like I feel, just knowin'
   that winter's gone for good,
When I see the rangeland grasses turnin' green.

He's not all bad—shore ain't no saint—
   but somewhere in the middle.
So don't label him a villain *or* a martyr.

He's a part of Mother Nature,
    same as all us human bein's,
But in a lot of ways, the coyote's smarter!

Ya see, he takes life day to day,
    don't waste no time with worryin',
Over what could be, or what just might go wrong.

That wily old coyote
    makes the best of what he has.
Maybe that's what he's been sayin' all along!

Just For One Time

Night visitors came calling while I slept,
   tracks show plainly in the dust outside.
Shrew and deer mouse, bobcat, and coyote,
   impressions left at dawn can't be denied.

Confined to cave and burrow through the day,
   escaping from the unrelenting heat
Of summer on the great Sonoran Desert,
   night is when antagonists must meet.

Though trails criss-cross,
   merge and meld together,
     they're neatly patterned; not in disarray.
So for at least this time,
   in this one place,
     last night it seems, they went their separate way.

"Cattle and man have a bond"

Desert Cowboy's Christmas

The bells this cowboy's hearin',
  aren't off of any sleigh.
They're 'round the necks of the old milk cows
  comin' in for their mornin' hay.

There've been other times and places,
  where there weren't snowflakes fallin',
But he can't remember a Christmas,
  when there weren't cattle bawlin'.

The desert air is chilled,
  as daylight tints the sky.
It's plenty cold enough for frost
  but the air is just too dry.

Against the graying pre-dawn
  there's a darker silhouette.
A remuda horse has just come in,
  but he can't tell which one yet.

The faint scent of creosote brush
  drifts on the mornin' breeze,
And prob'ly because of the day
  makes him think of Christmas trees.

Pausing, he watches the sunrise
  break the hold of the night.
Objects begin to emerge from the dark
  changing form in the light.

Saguaro, arms reaching skyward,
  cottonwood trees, bare limbed.
A rooster up on the big corral fence
  sittin' there crowin' at him.

An old cow begins to bawl,
  knowin' it's time for feed.
He breaks the bales and scatters the hay,
  and the others follow her lead.

Cattle and man have a bond,
  they've always been his life.
Over the years they've taken the place
  of a family and a wife.

As seasons follow seasons,
  he's never changed direction.
Horses, cattle, and wide-open spaces,
  the "cowboy connection".

"Merry Christmas, Girls," he calls,
  "here's a little extra hay.
An old cowboy likes to do his part
  to make this a special day!"

His Christmas seldom means presents,
  or bright lights on a tree,
More a time to pause and reflect
  on the way a man ought to be.

Some folks don't understand this,
  but it really isn't so strange.
It's what a cowboy's life's all about,
  to a shepherd of the range.

Attention Ranching and Farming Wives!

The following night school courses are now being offered for women, who are married to, or thinking of becoming, the wife of a cowboy, rancher, or farmer.

SELF IMPROVEMENT—

100—Creative Hairstyles

How to maintain a hairstyle that doesn't look like a bird's nest that blew out of a tree, while working in a dusty corral with a hat jammed on your head all day.

101—The Art Of Patience

Learn to quietly relax and ignore threats, violent gestures, and obscenities, while working with your mate during any ranch activity.

102—How To Dress For Company

Short cutting methods of changing from manure and dirt covered blue jeans, sweat shirt and boots, in the time it takes your minister to get the three-quarters of a mile from the highway to the house, after you see his car turn down your road.

103—How To Overcome Self-doubt

Learn ways to increase your awareness of what your husband, or "significant other" *actually* told you to do, and what he later *claims* he told you, when the whole thing gets screwed up.

HOME ECONOMICS—

200—Cast Your Bread Upon The Waters

This course consists of merely taking ingredients that you have on hand, such as half a dozen sprouting potatoes, left over pinto beans, a dozen molding tortillas, a pound of venison hamburger, and three shriveled hot dogs, and turning them into a respectable, though perhaps not gourmet, meal that will feed the two hungry men your husband just invited for dinner. (It's now 6:00 p.m. and you just came in from helping work cows all day.)

201—How To Utilize Your Kitchen Utensils For Vet Equipment

Discover the multiple uses of spatulas, strainers, scissors, colanders, basters, even pots and pans, as everyday barn/vet supplemental equipment, since your husband has usually misplaced the real items, or loaned them to a neighbor.

202—Cultivating Plant Growth In The Home

Turn your vast experience growing fungi and molds found in unidentifiable left-overs in your frig, into ways of keeping alive, for more than a week, even *one* potted plant.

203—Economical Ways To Stretch The Food Budget

Actually learn to prepare and cook (without showing signs of disgust) the "mountain oysters", rattlesnake, bear, ground hog, etc. that men have been known to bring home, proudly proclaiming, "If it's cooked right, it's delicious!"

HEALTH—

300—How To Maintain Your Correct Weight

Advice on how to grab a bite for *yourself* while preparing meals, serving, and cleaning up after haying crews, round-up crews, or any other kind of crews. Under this heading we will touch on places to hide cookies, cake, pie, candy, etc. where there'll be some left if you ever do get a chance to eat.

301—Pacing Yourself For Calmer Bathroom Moments

"How To" for allowing regular scheduled moments to yourself in the bathroom at least once a day, or if regular scheduling is totally out of the question, learning how to determine, within a few minutes, how long it will take before the "guys" get back with another bunch of cattle and will need the gate to be *open*.

BUSINESS AND CAREER—

400—How To Make $1000.00 Or More A Year Profit In Ranching

Tricks showing how to offset drought, disease, environmental constraints, deaths and market downswings in the farm and ranching business and come out ahead.

401—Expanding Your Options (See session 400 above)

Information on possibly extending your business to include llamas, emus, ostriches, or other exotics. With hard work and determination, they too, can show the same kind of profit as cattle and sheep.

402—Bookkeeping Tips

Learn ways to locate cancelled checks, receipts, tax statements, bills and other items given to your mate, when he can't remember where he put them, or that he ever had them. Additionally, we'll try to familiarize you with the latest methods of identifying what is written on the paper that was in his shirt pocket and went through the wash.

These classes will be given on Sunday between 11:00 p.m. and 3:00 a.m. "weakly," as this was deemed the most likely time women interested in these subjects could make the class.

Sign up on your next run to town for parts, when the tractor or well pump breaks down, you need welding rod, combiotics or vaccine from the vet, or you find the freezer totally void of meat because the dry cow you were going to butcher a month ago, calved.

Heifers on the Jarvis Ranch, Oregon

His Other Love

I knew of his obsession when we married,
    I knew it wasn't just a passing fling,
But I always thought his passion would diminish-
    but he's MORE devoted now, if anything!

So, I guess that even time will never change him,
    and although I'm sure he meant his wedding vows,
His pledge to love and honor, forsaking all others,
    in his cowboy's mind, did not extend to cows!

"Come on, we're burnin' daylight!"

A Cowdog's Day

The light just went on in the kitchen,
    and it's shinin' through my doghouse door.
I'll turn around and curl up tight,
    and maybe catch a few winks more.

Soon enough the boss will whistle,
    signalin' it's time to go.
Kinda hate to leave this old blanket—
    it's feelin' like ten below!

I can hear Cowboy tellin' his wife
    he'll be bringin' cows and calves in.
Said she wouldn't need to help out,
    he'd just take old Rin Tin Tin!

I *hate* it when he calls me that!
    I'm a cowdog, as anyone can see.
But, I guess it's probably better than
    "You blankety-blank S.O.B.!"

There he goes, headed out to the barn,
    I'm not about to get left behind!
He's tellin' me we've got cow work to do;
    somethin' neither of us mind!

I've stretched and shook out the kinks,
    baptized each bush and rock,
Kinda got myself all psyched up,
    ready to go lookin' for stock!

That ol' horse has a hump in his back,
    Boss better not get in a hurry.
I've seen that knothead buck pretty hard...
    oh what the heck, that's his worry!

There's the sun comin' up, good show!
    I'm startin' to get in the mood.
Scoutin' the country lookin' for cows,
    has changed my whole attitude!

Whoa! What's that commotion behind me?
    Shoot, that dang cowpony just blew!
Glue factory reject; he needs a lesson—
    and a chomp on the hock oughta do!

Take that you uncanned Alpo!
    I'll give ya' somethin' to buck about!
Look at him pitch through those snowdrifts,
    and listen to old Cowboy shout!

Why is he yellin' at me though?
    His partner, pal, man's best friend?
I help him out and get cussed for it—
    humans are hard to comprehend!

I got that cayuse lined out too,
    'course he's got one eye lookin' behind!
But I'm not wastin' more time on him,
    there's cows that I'm needin' to find.

And this canine nose just informed me,
 there's cattle a ways up the trail.
Cowboy said, "Go get around 'em, Jake!"
 so I'm really shakin' my tail!

Silly old heifers, you can't escape,
 I know all the tricks to this trade!
And there's no use tryin' to hook me,
 this super cowdog ain't afraid!

I'm here, then I'm there, like a flash,
 sure hope Boss is catchin' this show!
I've got those old girls turnin' now,
 headed home where we want 'em to go!

"Keep 'em comin', Jake," the Boss calls,
 that's my signal to grab some heels!
Whoopee ti yea! Look at 'em go,
 can't believe just how darn good that feels!

I work first one side, then the other,
 those calves better not try to lag.
They're only safe up with their mothers,
 when this heeler is workin' the drag!

The corrals are comin' in sight,
 we're back, with not a single snafu!
I'm sometimes amazed, what one lone cowboy,
 with a super cowdog can do!

He steps off his horse and pats my head,
 says, "Good job, old Rin Tin Tin."
I coulda got mad; but what's in a name?
 I just scratch at my collar, and grin!

"Dust covers the truck like a shroud"

Haulin' Water In Dry Times

As I sit watchin' the watertank fill,
　　with the generator's roar in my ears,
I think about rain and pray it comes early,
　　as the time of the monsoon nears.

The dirt tanks no longer have water,
　　only cracked mud that's curled and dried.
There hasn't been rain in over three months,
　　so the water for stock, we provide.

Every fourth day we fill up the tanker,
　　and haul water out to our cows.
Last winter rains produced plenty of grass,
　　so there's lots of old feed and browse.

It takes twenty minutes to fill the tank,
　　and another hour for the drive,
Where we wind our way over narrow dirt tracks,
　　with the load our cows need to survive.

The roads, from our travel, have turned to powder,
　　dust covers the truck like a shroud.
"My God we need rain!" my husband declares,
　　and echoes my own thoughts out loud.

There's no cattle at the drinkers today,
　　they've watered and moved out to graze.
We fill the supply tank, and check on the floats,
　　completing the last hauling phase.

Here the quail and the dove quench their thirst too,
    as do coyote, bobcat and deer.
They're seldom seen, but we know they're around,
    for the tracks in the dust are clear.

And I can't help but feel satisfaction,
    in knowin' that the water we haul,
Provides not only for cows, in dry times,
    but for all creatures great and small.

"*I can't help but feel satisfaction*"

"On the table was a tarnished silver frame"

The Silver Frame

It was in Montana's Gallatin Mountain Range
     on one cold October morning in the fall.
I was hunting for some remnants after roundup,
     knowing that we hadn't found 'em all.

When in a grove of quakin' aspens near a creek bed,
     I saw something that I hadn't seen before.
The edge of what appeared to be a rooftop,
     and the frame around a badly weathered door.

I reined my pony in and sat there squintin'
     thru shadows that the trees and thick brush cast.
Then my eyes discerned the outline of a cabin,
     a faded, rusting image from the past.

I stepped off my horse and started pushing through
     growth so dense it almost turned me back,
'Til I stumbled up against a rotted pine log,
     that once had been the step into the shack.

A packrat nest was lodged beside one corner
     of the doorway that gave access to the room.
I leaned my shoulder in and shoved against it,
     'til it opened and I stepped into the gloom.

As my eyes adjusted to the cabin's darkness,
     it was almost like I'd walked into the past.
With that musty smell of places long deserted,
     and cobweb veils that spiders had amassed.

In a corner sat a rusted metal bed frame,
    at one end a stove that once had furnished heat.
In the middle of the room a chair and table,
    where the long departed tenant sat to eat.

On the table in a tarnished silver frame,
    was a picture cloaked with dust from countless years.
As I picked it up and wiped the dingy glass,
    the faded photo of a girl appears.

She was lovely, with a dark cascade of curls,
    a girl in her late teens would be my guess.
And on the bottom of the picture had been written,
    "To my Jacob, all my love, from your Bess."

Then I noticed a yellowed piece of newsprint
    that was lying underneath the picture frame.
I carefully picked it up and started reading,
    it told of the derailment of a train.

It said many had been injured and two killed,
    that a full investigation would take place.
I looked again at the picture of the girl,
    with the Mona Lisa smile on her face.

The article was dated August fifth,
    and the year was nineteen hundred forty three.
The wreck took place near Salt Lake City, Utah.
    I felt a sudden chill come over me.

For I somehow knew the girl in that picture
    had been one of those aboard who died that day.
Was she coming to Montana to meet Jacob,
    or could it be that she had gone away?

I further searched the room, but found no clues
    as to who Jake was, or how long he'd been gone.
Just the mystery of a faded photograph,
    that a lovely girl named Bess had written on.

My horse's whinny broke in on my thoughts,
    and brought me back from sixty years before.
I replaced the frame and clipping on the table,
    then turned away and walked out of the door.

The brightness of the sun seemed an intrusion,
    and I quickly shut the door, and slid the bolt,
Made my way back through that tangled thicket,
    to where I'd tied and left my buckskin colt.

He was pawing, anxious to be going,
    I swung into the saddle and looked back.
The way the sun shown though those quakin' aspen,
    it looked almost like a halo 'round the shack.

I shivered, though the morning sun was warm,
    turned my horse toward where I'd left the trail.
I knew I'd need to make up time that morning,
    and I tried to think of cows, to no avail.

For my mind kept going back to those lovers,
    and the cabin that seemed almost like a shrine,
For a girl on the photo in a silver frame,
    and two lives from another place in time.

"How is he to ride?"

It's What's Left Unsaid!

There are horsetraders, and there are horsetraders. Asking questions and listening to their answers might seem to be a fairly logical and simple way of finding out about a horse you might consider buying. But be forewarned—what some of them say, and what they actually mean, can have a totally different interpretation. For instance—

QUESTION: "How is this horse about being caught?"

ANSWER: "Catch him anywhere."

(Interpretation) As long as he's hobbled and draggin' a twenty foot lead rope with a two hundred pound weight on the end.

QUESTION: "Is he easy to saddle?"

ANSWER: "No problem!"

(Interpretation) We just use a stripping chute, a blindfold, and tie up one foot.

QUESTION: "How is he to ride? Ever buck?"

ANSWER: "Naw, I doubt there's a buck in him!"

(Interpretation) Couldn't be, he used 'um all up last time he was rode.

QUESTION: "How about hauling?"

ANSWER: "Totally relaxed."

(Interpretation) He threw himself when we were trying to load him and laid down in the trailer all the way.

QUESTION: "How is he about guns?"

ANSWER: "He don't mind a gun at all."

(Interpretation) Just make sure it's never fired—at least within a mile of him.

QUESTION: "How is he to shoe?"

ANSWER: "Heck, he just hands his feet to you."

(Interpretation) Especially the hind ones, with the thrust of a rocket engine.

QUESTION: "Can I bring him back if he doesn't work out?"

ANSWER: "If he ain't just like I said him to be, you don't have to own him!"

(Interpretation) Of course, what I *said*, and how you interpreted it, means "Lady, he's YOURS!"

Photo by Lee Raine

He just needs a little work.

"Spring-fed ponds in every draw"

Water, Cows, and Grass

It's water, cows, and grass
    that fill a rancher's dreams.
Cattle standin' belly deep,
    in a wavin' sea of green.

Spring-fed ponds in every draw,
    where cattails hug the bank,
Or some old creakin' windmill,
    fillin' up the water tank.

There's nothin' looks no better,
    or gives a man more ease,
Than an old cow full of water,
    in grass up to her knees!

"*Wood and stone still mark the place*"

The Heritage

Four generations ranched this land,
    two are buried here.
Wood and stone still mark the place
    they've rested through the years.

Grandpa brought his new bride
    a century ago,
To homestead on the bottomlands,
    where clear sweet waters flow.

They raised three boys to manhood,
    but one went hunting gold,
Another left to serve the Lord,
    just one stayed in the fold.

In time that one son married
    a girl named Emily.
They built a home and raised four kids,
    and one of them was me.

We grew up knowin' cattle
    from their bawlin' to their brand,
And Dad instilled his rancher's pride
    and feelings for the land.

Keep the fences mended,
    give your best, was what he asked.
Never break another's trust
    or let an anger last.

Hard work was just one measure
    of how he judged a man.
If his horse had savvy,
    what kind of bulls he ran.

Mama had her own ideas,
    but seldom made them known.
Her time was mostly occupied
    in managing our home.

And I guess we took for granted
    our life out on the range,
But we grew up and they grew old,
    and things began to change.

Destiny, it seemed, had plans
    that no one could foresee.
My sister moved away to teach,
    John died at Normandy.

That left Justin and myself
    who made the choice to stay,
And we were living on the ranch
    when both folks passed away.

Though the world and times keep changing,
    the cows still wear *our* brand,
And our kids grew up on horseback,
    and learned to love this land.

We're a family grateful for this life,
    and what freedom it still allows.
Each generation passing on
    its heritage of cows.

*Carole and Dan's daughters Laura and Dannalee on the
homeplace near Wickenburg, 1963.*

"And the episode was done"

The Stranger

The summer heat was stifling,
    as he parked his pickup truck,
In front of the only bar in town,
    called Little Bit O' Luck.

A cold beer and a chance to stretch
    in a place he'd never been,
Then two more hours to Wickenburg,
    and he'd be home again.

Cowboy boots, hat and jeans,
    a slim-fit denim shirt;
No urban cowboy this one,
    ranching was his work.

He stepped inside the darkened room
    and let his eyes adjust,
Then sat down on a bar stool,
    "A beer, to cut the dust."

He tipped the glass of cold beer,
    smiled and breathed a sigh.
"That really takes the edge off.
    Lord, but I was dry!"

The only other person
    in the tavern at the time,
Was one old man the stranger guessed
    was down to his last dime.

He sat talkin' of the old days,
    the way it used to be.
To no one in particular,
    just one man's reverie.

"There ain't no heroes anymore,"
    the old man shook his head.
"That's what we need, are heroes,
    but all of them are dead!

Yes sir, those men who weren't afraid
    of nothin' on this earth.
You couldn't set no value,
    what one of them was worth!"

His weathered face half hidden,
    by gray-white beard and hat,
The pale blue eyes were hard to see
    from where the stranger sat.

"Bartender, bring my friend a beer,
    and one more glass for me."
The stranger nodded toward the man,
    "Guess you're not drinkin' tea?"

The old man shifted on his stool,
    and turned around to stare.
Until right then he hadn't known
    that someone else was there.

"Well no sir, beer will shore be fine,"
    he raised his glass in toast.
"I thank ya'" then his face turned white,
    as if he'd seen a ghost.

The stranger stood to move,
    when he heard a clicking sound,
That raised the hair up on his neck.
    He slowly turned around.

Standing by the barman,
    whose eyes were wide with fear,
A big man held a pistol,
    pointed right behind his ear.

"Just keep it cool," he ordered,
    "unless you want to die!
Put yer money on the bar."
    He never blinked an eye.

"Open up that cash drawer
    and dump it in this sack.
You two pass yer wallets up,
    and don't play hero, Mac!"

His eyes fixed on the cowboy,
    the gunman seemed aware
If there was any trouble
    it would likely come from there.

The barman's hands were shaking
   as he emptied out the drawer,
Then bent to pick the money up
   he'd spilled across the floor.

Distracted for a minute,
   the robber looked away.
It was now or never
   and the stranger made his play.

Sheer momentum drove him,
   and the gunman hit the floor,
The pistol flew across the room
   and slid against the door.

The robber sat there, dazed,
   as the stranger grabbed the gun,
Had the barman call the sheriff,
   and the episode was done.

And the cowboy, like the old days,
   seemed to take it all in stride.
He really never thought about
   the fact he might have died.

When he left the little bar,
   he was barely out of sight,
Before the whole town learned about,
   the stranger and the fight.

He would have been surprised, at best,
    to know he'd left a mark.
His main concern was makin' it
    to Wickenburg by dark.

But maybe things do happen
    according to some plan,
Like resurrecting heroes
    for the dreams of one old man.

"Livin' the cowboy dream"

Lovin' The Life They're Livin'

There's laughter out in the dining room
    and I pause in what I'm doin',
And smile, and think about those boys
    who'll be drinkin' this coffee I'm brewin'.

There's buckaroos Luther and Corky,
    young Randy from up near Cheyenne,
Deacon, he "jiggers" the outfit,
    gray-haired Mike, who they call the Old Man.

They rode out before dawn lit the sky,
    and rode back as darkness closed in.
After all those hours in the saddle,
    you'd think humor would wear pretty thin.

But Corky is hammerin' on Luther,
    about missin' "a plumb easy throw",
And Mike adds, "You need a faster horse,
    or ya' better start tellin' cows whoa!"

And Randy, who barely has whiskers,
    well, he's takin' a lot of flak too.
Seems the tall leggy colt he's been ridin'
    scattered cattle three ways when he blew.

As I bring in the pot of coffee,
    their banter gets kinda subdued.
The grins on their faces still linger—
    but they don't want me thinkin' 'em rude.

85

These cowboys are gentlemen, always,
    when they come in the ranchhouse to eat.
Their hats are hung up in the hallway,
    at the door, each one wiped his feet.

"Grab your cups boys, the coffee's boiled twice!"
    I say as I set the pot down.
"There's roast beef, potatoes and gravy,
    and the biscuits are just about brown."

Young Randy, smilin' broadly declares,
    "I could eat my own horse and his hide!"
Corky, with a loud chuckle, answers,
    "He's prob'ly easier to eat than to ride!"

Randy's face flushed, bein' reminded,
    how his colt came unwound that day,
Buckin' thru cows they'd just gathered,
    causin' more than a little delay.

"You cowboys sit down," I tell 'em,
    "I'm sure the biscuits are done."
Deacon takes his place next to Randy,
    and with a grin says, "Don't worry, Son."

"You did a good job with that pony,
    there was no daylight under your seat.
These boys have all been there and done that,
    so pay 'em no mind and let's eat."

I've set the food out on the table,
    and five hungry cowhands dig in.
They've put in a long hard day workin',
    and their waistlines have grown mighty slim.

Back in the kitchen I slice the pies,
    and put on more coffee to brew.
Once in a while I catch a few words
    of conversation from the crew.

The tone of their voices has softened,
    content, now their bellies are full.
They're workin' out plans for tomorrow,
    I hear talk of cows and the bull.

This time of night is for strategy,
    and reviewin' events of the day.
Deacon, checkin' his tallybook,
    asks Mike about brands on a stray.

Then supper is through, and hats retrieved,
    and with thank yous, I'm bid goodnight.
Soon their voices fade in the distance
    and silhouettes vanish from sight.

Sleep will be all too brief for these hands,
    they'll be ridin' by dawn's first gleam,
But short nights and long days don't matter,
    'cause they're livin' the cowboyin' dream.

"There'll be no turnin' loose 'til he's all done!"

Those Maverick-Chasin' Mavericks

Some folks think the Wild West days are over,
    but the fact is, there's some places still untamed,
And in the very roughest, toughest landscape,
    many a wild cow critter's yet unclaimed.

Where chaparral is thick and dense they scatter,
    steep canyons rise above to form a wall.
A maverick bull could hide in spittin' distance,
    but unless he moves, you won't see him at all.

They've never felt a rope or brandin' iron,
    no knife has ever notched a single ear.
And since their mamas weaned 'em off the teat,
    there's been no cowboy ever has come near.

By two years old they're smart as any mustang;
    they disappear 'neath catclaw and mesquite.
Even with a bunch of good wild cow dogs,
    gettin' them unbrushed can be a feat!

If you're lucky and the dogs do bring 'em out,
    they'll be mad as hell and lookin' for a fight,
And a thousand pounds of furious maverick bull,
    could get the toughest cowhand in a tight!

Now if you're thinkin' all this sounds real "hairy",
    well partner, the work has just begun.
'Cause once he's got his rope tied to that critter,
    there'll be no turnin' loose 'til he's all done!

But here in Arizona there are cowboys,
    some say you have to see, to believe.
As wild a ridin', maverick-ropin' hombres,
    as ever laid a rope upon a beeve!

They toss their loop from any damn direction,
    left or right, ahead of them, behind.
And few there are, who's ever seen 'um miss one—
    they work plumb magic with a length of twine!

They're out before the gray dawn barely shows,
    followin' on the tracks of some wild cow
Who's always found a place to hide her calf,
    so never one's been branded, up 'til now.

For she, herself, was born out in this country
    she knows each rock and cranny, knob and knoll.
Where to find the grass when feed is scanty,
    the distance from each muddy waterhole.

Her skill at disappearin' like a shadow,
    won't save her now—these boys aren't like the rest.
They'll bed her down before this day is over—
    she's goin' to a brandin'—as the guest!

And when she's roped, jerked down a time or two,
    he'll tie her feet before she gets her wind,
Truss her like a turkey on Thanksgiving,
    then saw her horns off, back where they begin.

He'll let her lay 'til she gives up the battle,
    agreein' to be led, 'longside his horse.
Snubbed up close, the rope around her horn stubs,
    she really hasn't got much choice, of course.

So if you're in the Arizona "outback,"
    and happen on wild cattle tied to trees,
Where there are signs of some tremendous battles,
    and those critters kinda look like refugees,

You've run onto the work of maverick catchers,
    and few there are, who have what this job takes.
Absolutely fearless, savvy horsemen,
    in a venture where there's room for few mistakes.

They know they're riskin' life and limb and horse,
    and for all the sweat, the wage is mighty slim.
But there's compensation in another way,
    like the satisfaction when they lead 'em in.

Mustang

He stands there alone, on the top of a ridge,
    a sentinel, testing the air.
Nothing below him but sagebrush and sand,
    yet some instinct bids him beware.

Hard lessons have taught him over the years
    what it takes to just stay alive.
An unsympathetic world is his,
    in the struggle to merely survive.

The tips of both ears have been frozen off,
    and he's narrow between the eyes.
All muscle and bone and sinew and heart,
    the ruggedness "mustang" implies.

Life hasn't been easy, one glance will tell—
    his black hide is covered with scars.
White dapples of hair in all shapes and sizes,
    like a night sky speckled with stars.

Born in the wilds to an old outlaw mare,
    with a feral range stud for a sire.
His heritage gave him the skills to survive
    the cougar, and man, and barb wire.

He knows where a seep forms a small pool,
    precious water on long summer days.
Knows of a place where rocks make a shade
    from the worst of the sun's scorching rays.

He's outlasted winter, facing starvation
    when icy storms raged and blew.
Pawed out the snow in search of dried grasses
    that gave him the strength to get through.

Another season, another year gone,
    and the earth shows promise of spring.
Over and over he whinnies a challenge,
    'til the canyons behind him ring.

But he's answered only with silence,
    and he lowers his head and moves on.
With just the eyes of a hawk above him
    to even know that he's gone.

"He stands there alone, on the top of a ridge"

Payin' Attention

"**I** told ya' once, it's the second gate,
    and leave the dang thing *open*!
Close the one with the fingertrap;
    that's where they'll water—I'm hopin'.

Now pay attention; watch fer cows;
    make sure the fences are up.
Keep yer mind on what we're doin' out here,
    and quit lookin' fer buttercup!"

Then off he rides in a cowboy trot,
    his eyes on the trail up ahead.
And me, I'm tryin' to concentrate,
    on all of the things he just said.

But above me there's a red-tail hawk,
    and I watch him circle and soar.
Then into the wind he dips and turns,
    with the grace of a matador!

And what made those tracks in the wash;
    they're not rabbit or coyote I know,
But some kind of critter wandered this way,
    and it hasn't been that long ago.

Guess I really shouldn't tarry though,
    so come on old horse, let's get goin'.
I'm sure by now Dan's halfway there,
    and I'd better be a-showin'.

Okay, this trail is headed right,
    and I can see all the fence from here.
Gee, what a lovely day for a ride,
    oh wow, there's a herd of mule deer!

With three or four does and a buck,
    a couple of spikes! Boy they're quick!
Over that ridge and out of sight
    like kids on a pogo stick!

That buck was a five-point, at least!
    I wonder where he hid last fall?
Wherever it was, I hope he goes back—
    uh oh, I think I heard a cow bawl!

Oh nuts, that came from way up ahead—
    I pray they're not through the gate!
Come on little horse, let's hit a lope,
    I'm in big trouble if I'm too late!

And there they are, headin' straight in
    toward the gate I'm supposed to close!
At a dead run now, it's nip and tuck—
    and I beat 'um—but just by a nose!

Wow! That was too close, old pony,
    I'd never hear the end of that,
If they'd gotten through and scattered...
    well, let's go see where the rest are at.

Here comes Dan now with the big bunch,
    ridin' in from the other direction.
"Good", he says, when he sees these cows,
    "looks like ya' paid attention!"

I always do, I say to him,
    and a laugh is his reaction.
Just because on a rare occasion,
    I might have had a distraction.

So I tell him the fence is all up,
    and there's plenty of feed in the draw.
But I keep to myself, all the other things,
    that when I paid attention I saw!

Daughter Laura "payin' attention."

"The two horses scrambled and lunged"

The Phantom Trail

The storm clouds had gathered since morning,
  in the distance she heard thunder roll.
Urging her mare to a gallop,
  they topped yet another small knoll.

The rain was still back on the mountain,
  but the ranch was an hour away,
And the dark clouds seemed to be closing
  in a threatening kind of way.

Rosa stopped at the edge of a bluff
  just as lightning flashed in the sky.
She'd have to find a quicker way home
  for any chance to stay dry.

Below stretched a deep sandy wash,
  maybe fifteen or twenty feet wide,
Dry, with a scattering of boulders
  where she just might put time on her side.

As she started down over the edge
  the little horse plunged and slid,
Frantically trying to stay on her feet,
  rolling gravel and rocks as she did.

When they finally reached the bottom,
  Rosa turned and rode up the draw.
The mare snorted and tossed her head,
  the wind had quickly turned raw.

"Come on, *mi caballo*," she spoke,
  "we still have a long way to go.
If this wash runs into the Santa Maria,
  we can cut off five miles I know!"

On each side the big rocks grew steeper,
  while the sky above darkened and growled.
She found herself in a deep canyon,
  where the captive wind shrieked and howled.

Rosa shuddered and pulled her hat tight,
  gave thanks for the jacket she'd worn,
When somewhere beyond, in the canyon,
  a sound on the wind was borne.

Vague, like the dim muffle of thunder,
  yet the rumbling didn't end.
She stopped and listened intently—
  what threat lay around that bend?

Then suddenly instinct took over,
  and she whirled her mare with a yell,
Spurred her back the way they'd come,
  as though chased by demons from hell!

She knew now the danger she faced,
  knew now that thundering sound.
Somehow she had to climb these rocks
  and make it to higher ground!

The wind brought a trace of rain
    and the faint smell of mud.
Behind like some living thing,
    rolled water, and rock and flood!

As in vain she searched for a trail—
    a way to escape up the side,
A rider appeared, out of nowhere,
    shouted, "Follow me—and RIDE!"

Without the least hesitation,
    she laid her quirt to the mare,
Raced alongside the lone rider
    to a spot where the rocks formed a stair.

Up went the horse with his rider,
    scaling the face of the wall,
Behind him Rosa's mare followed,
    as a hard rain began to fall.

The two horses scrambled and lunged,
    yet it all seemed in slow motion,
While below swept a surge of water,
    like a tidal wave from an ocean.

She clung desperately to her mare,
    'til at last they reached the top.
Only then did she turn and look down
    at that sheer, vertical drop.

As she'd raced ahead of the torrent,
    she'd known her life was in danger,
But now she realized, she would have died,
    if it hadn't been for the stranger.

"*Gracias, Amigo*," she smiled at him,
    and the young vaquero smiled back.
"I'd never have seen that trail," she said,
    "why it's hardly more than a track!"

"*Sí, Señorita*," he answered,
    "there are few ever come this way.
My grandfather found it some years ago,
    when he was following a stray."

"Who is your grandfather, *señor?*" she asked,
    "and please, what is your name?"
"His name is Jose de Anza," he spoke,
    "and I was called the same."

"My name is Rosa Alonso," she told him,
    "and this is part of our ranch.
Thank God you came along when you did,
    or I would never have had a chance.

"What can I do to repay you?" she urged,
    as the sun broke through a cloud.
"*Señorita*, the payment was made,
    when I saw you to safety," he vowed.

"And now I must say, adios;
    just follow this trail to your right.
It winds to the flatland below,
    and your rancho will soon be in sight."

He tipped his hat, spun his horse,
    and before she had time to reply,
The dashing vaquero was gone—
    as quick as the blink of an eye.

Below, the water still roared,
    and she hastily turned toward home,
Glanced the direction he'd taken,
    but she was there all alone.

By the time she dropped off the rim,
    the clouds had pulled back toward the west.
In the distance a rider appeared,
    that would be her padre, she guessed.

She galloped her mare toward the man,
    and heard him call out her name.
The relief on the face of her father
    made Rosa flush with shame.

"You worried me half to death," he said,
    "when the creeks began to flood!
The Santa Maria is raging,
    filled with debris and mud!"

"Yes Father, I know," she began,
    and told her story in detail.
He sat there, silently listening,
    but his face went deathly pale.

"So you see, Father, my life was saved
    by Jose de Anza," she said.
"I know you'll want to thank him yourself.
    How far are we from their spread?"

Her father stepped off his horse
    and looked up at his daughter's face.
"Rosa," he said, "this rancho,
    is part of the de Anza place.

"One hundred and fifty years ago,
    as far as the eye could see,
The family of Jose de Anza,
    was given this land, by decree.

There are stories of these rancheros,
    and the thousands of cattle they raised.
Of vaqueros who rode like Comanches,
    and watched over the land where they grazed.

And the story is told of one grandson,
    who was Jose's pride and joy.
They shared the same name and affection,
    from the time he was just a boy.

Of a day in the middle of summer,
    when a flash flood tore through this land.
How the elder de Anza escaped up a cliff
    where most horses couldn't stand.

But the boy didn't make it in time—
    horse and rider were swept away.
The waters receded by nighttime,
    and his body was found the next day.

On the hill overlooking that trail,
    he was laid to rest, it is told.
August eleventh, nineteen-o-three,
    the day he turned eighteen years old."

As her father finished his story,
    Rosa turned and looked back toward the hill.
Against an indigo blue sky,
    time, it seemed, just stood still.

She said, "My life was saved today, Father,
    when I was led up that trail of tears,
By a handsome vaquero on horseback,
    you say has been dead ninety years.

Perhaps what I met was angel,
    or a ghost from a time long ago.
But he was as real as you or I,
    This is one thing that I know.

So tomorrow I'll bring a red rose,
    and plant it on top of that rim,
In tribute to Jose de Anza,
    and the still-living spirit of him."

Nature's Bounty

To a cattleman, rancher, or cowboy, no discussion between friends, or even strangers, would be complete unless the topic of rain, or the lack thereof, was addressed. For without enough moisture, grasses that livestock need to survive and thrive, just don't grow. Which means that either hay or supplements must be fed to the animals, or they must be sold. Neither option is one a cowman wants to be put in a position to choose.

Generally, the first thing a cowboy does when he leaves the house in the morning is to check the sky for clouds. It is as much a part of a cowboy's ritual as catching and saddling his horse. And, when after a frequently experienced dry spell, a rainstorm drenches the earth with the long awaited moisture, the cowboy, in his own way, gives his thanks.

Thanks For The Rain

I turned my eyes toward cloudless skies
so often, Lord,
just searchin' for some sign or scent of rain.

Sometimes thinkin' that I heard
the sound of thunder,
far away, across some distant plain.

I watched the watertanks
turn into mudholes,
saw grasses dry and wither in the sun.

Stirred a trail of dust
behind my pony,
and dreamed each night the summer rains had come.

Then this mornin' when I woke,
I felt a change,
and lookin' toward the west, clouds filled the sky.

Soon the lightnin'
and the boom of thunder,
combined with rain to form a lullaby.

And no one knows
no better than a cowboy,
what moisture means to life in this terrain.

And though I know
You always planned to send it,
I had to tell you Lord,

THANKS FOR THE RAIN.

Dan in Oregon.

"I've got me a gentle, fourteen-two horse"

Not A Man's Problem

When I was younger, and a lot more agile,
    and lived where the winters were mild,
I never minded a big tall horse,
    or one that got easily riled.

But up north, where the winters are cold,
    where it snows, and it blows, and you freeze,
I've got me a gentle, fourteen-two horse,
    and my stirrups let out to his knees!

'Cause up in that far North Country,
    before venturing out in the cold,
I've put on so many layers of clothes,
    my body will hardly unfold!

First comes my long-johns and wool socks,
    then a quilted shirt and blue jeans.
A sweater and coat, on top of all this,
    and a slicker, of course, is routine.

Chaps or chinks are a must,
    leather gloves all lined inside,
Cowboy boots and overshoes,
    my head covered; then I can ride!

When the temperature hovers at thirty,
    and the wind is whippin' the snow,
The house feels so warm and cozy inside,
    Lord knows I'm not wantin' to go.

But that cowboy heads for the door,
    the horses are ready to haul.
Draggin' my boots won't do any good,
    it's no use tryin' to stall!

There's one last bunch of cows to move,
    and a storm came in overnight.
Yesterday, not one little cloud,
    the skies were sunny and bright.

So this change in the weather demands
    that my morning be totally free
Of any kind of liquids—
    no breakfast coffee for me!

'Cause the last thing in the world I need,
    and the thing I dread most of all,
Is gettin' dressed up in all of these clothes,
    then havin' to heed nature's call.

I try movin' out of the wind,
    but it follows wherever I go.
And when I'm finally down to bare skin,
    it's feelin' like twenty below!

My chaps are now 'round my ankles,
    my jeans somewhere 'neath my knees.
My longjohns won't go any lower,
    as I squat in the lee of some trees!

The wind blows the snow—and everything else—
    but you can't move, hobbled like that!
To even get up, you're so stiff from the cold,
    you need to be half-acrobat!

I had to take off my gloves
    to get undone for this feat,
And by now my fingers are so darn numb,
    the buckles and buttons won't meet!

By the time I get put back together,
    and make my way up on my horse,
The cowboy is bringin' the last of the cows,
    looking' plumb disgusted, of course!

Bein' a man, he can't figure,
    what would cause this long a delay.
In the meantime, I'll just keep workin',
    on learnin' to "hold it" all day!

Jarvis Ranch, Forepaugh, Arizona

The Home Ranch

It's not much for fancy, as home places go,
  the road comin' in is just dirt.
The outbuildings need a little repair,
  and a new coat of paint wouldn't hurt.

But the yard has green trees you notice for miles,
  and fences all up in good shape,
With a big lodgepole entrance into the place,
  that kinda frames the whole landscape.

A sign hangs from the top, cut out of metal,
  with the name of the ranch and its brand,
And you find yourself thinkin', whoever lives here,
  takes a lot of pride in their land.

The clack of the tires across the cattleguard,
  announce your coming and going.
Plus, two Heeler-crosses alert the whole ranch,
  by the noisy fit that they're throwing.

An American flag hangs on a tall pole,
  ruffling just a bit in the breeze,
On the front of the house is a big screened-in porch,
  half shaded by two of the trees.

It could be in Montana or Idaho,
  any place that ranching survives.
Where cattle are raised and families nurtured,
  and a proud way of life still thrives.

The sandhills of Nebraska, Utah's red rocks,
    Arizona's wide-open ranges,
The state will be different, and the name on the gate,
    but the rites and the life never changes.

For the same winds that blow 'neath Montana's Big Sky,
    chase tumbleweeds over the plains,
And rumbling storm clouds, heavy with moisture,
    for all, bring the same welcome rains.

Life out there means cattle, and horses and land,
    and ranchers who still meet the test,
Because somewhere, ever, even as today,
    they remain the soul of the west.

"An American flag hangs on a tall pole"

"A bunkhouse without any frills"

He Goes By The Name Of "Cowboy"

The last job I had, wasn't all that bad,
 'til the boss quit runnin' cows.
When we gathered that fall, he sold 'em all,
 and replaced 'em with fifty sows.

He asked would I stay, I answered "No way!"
 (hogs are unnatural critters).
They squeal, and stink, and their hides are all *pink*,
 and their youngun's come in litters!

You can't work 'em horseback, and a neck they lack,
 so how would ya' ever rope one?
Roundups are out, and without any doubt,
 to gather hogs, you'd need a gun!

So I made myself clear, I was not stayin' here,
 to turn into a "SOWboy".
I still have my pride, and I can still ride,
 and I'll end my years as a COWboy!

He paid me my wage, and I checked the gas gauge,
 on my trusty old sixty-nine Ford,
Tossed my bedroll in, and with a wide grin,
 put the pedal to the floorboard.

I took my own advice, as to not thinkin' twice,
 about where I'd find my next job,
Long as it's "swine-free," and there's no one but me,
 and my blue heeler sidekick, old Bob.

When next I hired on, for a outlaw named John,
    'twas a ranch way back in the hills.
An Ace Reid sort of place, with plenty of space,
    and a bunkhouse without any frills.

Here the prickly pear is as thick as the hair
    on a bearded lady's chin,
And boulders and rocks, cover bottoms and tops
    of each craggy draw and rim.

It's rough country to ride, and the man hadn't lied
    when he told me I'd earn my pay.
Ridin' herd on wild cows that live mainly on browse;
    starvation rations, I'd say.

I won't kid you none, it ain't what you call fun,
    spendin' long days in the saddle,
Where seldom is heard, an encouragin' word,
    'cause there's nobody out here but cattle,

And varmints and snakes- the mean kind that makes
    a rattlin' noise when I ride near,
Causin' heartbeat increase and breathin' to cease,
    and sometimes my pony to rear.

But that big Diamondback will end up in the sack
    tied to the strings on my saddle.
A whole lot dead and minus his head,
    he'll become a hatband with rattle.

'Cause those dudes in town like a hat with a crown
    tall enough for a wide snakeskin band,
And I've earned a twenty, darn easy money,
    for every snakehide that I've tanned.

What a cowboy gets paid, is like a Band-Aid®
    when yer life blood's seepin' away.
It might keep ya' alive, but ya' barely survive,
    and ain't real sure about the next day.

Then I think, what the heck, I get a paycheck,
    and there's some things money can't buy.
A cowboy's life's free, and the only PIG I see,
    is the breakfast bacon I fry.

"When an old cow makes her move I'm ready"

Round-Up Hand

It's still dark at five A.M. in mid-October,
　　and so cold it makes my toes and fingers ache.
The horses are all saddled and they're ready;
　　we'll be ridin' after cows by daybreak.

Last night my husband asked, "You wanna cowboy?
　　We can use an extra hand if you do."
"You bet!" I answered, figurin' it an honor,
　　bein' asked to help on round-up with that crew!

I'm teamed with four good cowboys and the cowboss,
　　and I listen close as he tells us who rides where.
I don't know this country half as well as they do,
　　and as I tighten up my cinch, I say a prayer.

'Cause I'll never make the Cowgirl Hall of Fame;
　　my catch rope kinda looks like wet spaghetti.
But I try to keep my horse and me positioned,
　　so when an old cow makes her move, I'm ready.

And we turn back most of those cantankerous cows,
　　but every now and then there's one gets by.
Chargin' like a freight train on the downhill—
　　her tail up in the air, plumb on the fly!

We're off, old Rose and me, but can't outrun her,
　　'cause she's got it in her mind she won't be penned.
Straight up the side of some steep rocky hill,
　　where badger holes are layin' end to end!

123

With only puffs of dust to mark her passing,
  she disappears in seconds from my view.
It's times like this I wish I *was* a cowboy,
  so I could show that cow a thing or two!

A cowboy's always mounted on some top horse,
  that turns and cuts and runs uphill with ease.
And if by some off chance a cow gets by him,
  he'll have her roped and back, slick as you please.

Well heck, my mare and me we do our best,
  and I know we've shortened up a lot of days.
Took a little pressure off the cowboys,
  even with our unprofessional ways.

And I sure don't mind not bein' called to rope one.
  I'm content bringin' pairs out to be tagged,
Or lettin' through the gate the ones they've doctored,
  (unless it's that old heavy gate that's sagged!)

Just gettin' out in time to catch a sunrise,
  as the first long rays descend across a hill.
Feelin', more than hearin', all the quiet,
  accompanyin' the mornin's predawn chill.

Coyotes speak their ancient coyote language,
  their hunt for food begun before the dawn.
Fair warnin' to the rabbits and the ground squirrels,
  when they hear that ageless old coyote's song.

In fall, the colors changin' day by day—
   greens replaced with yellow, red and gold.
Time to wean the calves off from the cows now;
   they're big and strong and almost eight months old.

If you've never been around at weanin' time,
   when they separate about three hundred pair,
You really can't imagine all the noise,
   that comes from cattle bawlin' everywhere.

The trucks arrive and haul the calves away,
   and still the old cows stand around and bawl.
You have to raise your voice up to a yell,
   or there's no way you'll be heard at all.

The day's been long and Rose and I are weary,
   but we held our end up, like the cowboy crew.
And I'll go to sleep tonight rememberin',
   when the cowboss smiled at me and said,
                    "You'll do!"

The First Sure Signs Of Spring

Out where the open prairie spreads wide,
  and the wind makes sagebrush sing,
The snow has pulled back to the hills—
  it's the first sure sign of spring.

There was extra hair in the currycomb
  when I saddled my horse at dawn.
And along the creek behind the barn,
  the ice is finally gone.

As the morning sky turned a pastel tint,
  I heard a familiar old call.
Canada geese passed right overhead,
  the first ones I've seen since last fall.

The old mama cat just had kittens,
  and the ewes are about to lamb.
Our milk cow, Grace, had her calf last week;
  the kids named him Abraham.

As the buds swell on the willow trees,
  and I spot the first springtime flower,
I'm aware these are indicators;
  winter is relinquishing power.

Which is fine, I'm tired of shoveling snow,
  and I'm glad for more daylight hours.
They help cut down on the loads of wood,
  our faithful old stove devours.

But even without all the other signs,
   I'd know spring has arrived once more,
By the pile of mud-covered overshoes,
   we put on and take off at the door!

When Dan turned 65, he asked me if I would write a poem especially for him, to commemorate this milestone. The following is the result.

The Sum Of His Parts

Guess my days as a top hand are through,
'Cause there sure ain't much left I can do.
    With two brand new knees,
        I kinda walk by degrees,
And how to run, I haven't a clue.

When temperatures fall below freezin',
Seems my lungs they start in to wheezin'.
    So the Doc says, "Stay in."
        And to my chagrin,
I've got where I find that real pleasin'!

My appendix and gall bladder's gone,
Seems half of my parts have been sawn.
    They chipped bone spurs away,
        Said my teeth had decay,
And I'd sure better watch when I yawn!

With a body that's stove-up so much,
There's no ropin' or round-ups and such.
    Why to get on my horse,
        I'd need a stepstool, of course,
And a place on my hull for my crutch!

Guess my memory ain't so good anymore,
And it's gettin' kinda hard to ignore.
    I have trouble at times,
        Rememberin' my rhymes;
What comes after and what comes before!

But I still wear my boots and my hat,
And guess that I'm lucky at that.
    Livin' out in the West,
    On the land I love best,
Where the rest of the cowboys are at!

And the ladies still give me the eye
When they see my red pickup drive by.
    'Cause this cowboy antique,
    Still has cowboy mystique,
And I hope *that part* lasts, 'til I die!

"To look from a knoll, down into a basin"

Dan and I collaborated on the writing of this poem. We combined memories from over the years.

Thumbin' Back Through The Pages Of Life's Book

A band of wild horses, untamed and free,
　　pause on the skyline to look my way,
Then disappear down the other side,
　　and turn my thoughts back to yesterday.

Rememberin' another bunch of mustangs-
　　sorrels and roans and one blood-red bay.
How three reckless lads captured them all—
　　oh, to be young again, just for today!

To look from a knoll, down into a basin,
　　watchin' young calves frolic and play.
Range-wise old cows keep a careful eye—
　　ah, to be a cowboy, again for a day.

Ridin' out through a meadow, early in spring;
　　there's a sow bear with cubs, makin' their way.
One little dark one and one almost gold—
　　a sight to remember for a cowboy that day.

I see the trout risin', harvestin' May-flies,
　　that swarm over water as the dawn turns gray.
Rememberin' the taste of a pan-fried Rainbow—
　　what I'd give to go back, just for a day.

Once again hearin' the wind in the pine trees,
    and watchin' the tops, as in rhythm they sway.
Listen to creakin' trunk against trunk—
    Lord put me back there, just for one day.

Let me wind down the trail of a canyon,
    announced by the screech of a jay.
See his flash of blue close above me—
    be that lone rider, just for a day.

To listen from camp for the sound of the bell horse,
    hear a low nicker, and the pack mule's bray.
Go to sleep lulled by the sounds in the darkness—
    oh, take me back there, if only one day.

Fall colors that dazzle, late Indian summer,
    a bugling bull elk, only minutes away.
I rein in my horse and wait for an answer—
    make me that cowboy again for a day.

The cows are all followin' my creakin' old wagon,
    stoppin' to feed as I throw out their hay.
Snow piled high and glistenin' like diamonds—
    scenes that make memories last more than a day.

Of those years spent on horseback, carin' for cows,
    I wouldn't have changed even one yesterday.
'Cause I've known the freedom that few others know
    livin' my life in the real cowboy way.

Though my step has slowed, my body grown tired,
   and my brown hair turned mostly to gray,
I still have the book, with all of the pages,
   to make me that cowboy, again for a day.

Photo by Shell Beck

Carole and Dan "Makin' memories." DG Ranch, Arizona

Winter Years

He still has the spark in his eye, but you have to be knowledgeable about cowboys to see it. It tends to come and go. When unfamiliar people surround him and in unfamiliar places, he withdraws into himself and the spark withdraws into his subconscious. Let him out on a prairie with open sky and horizons uncluttered with cities or housing developments and the spark returns, and his back straightens, and his step gets lighter.

Looking at him now, it wouldn't be obvious to most people, what a top hand he had been. How proudly he sat a horse. He was handsome and slim in the days of his youth, muscular and tanned to an acorn brown from years of hard work and life out in the sun and wind.

He could throw a loop that would fly as true as an arrow, and his eyes were sharp enough to read a cow's brand from as far away as he could tell a heifer from a steer.

Now he spins out a yarn, like he spun out a loop. His last horse is retired to pasture, his old dog died last winter, and some of the town people keep asking him whenever he's in town, if he doesn't want to come in to the Senior Center and meet some new people.

Isn't it lonely out there, they ask? He politely answers no; he never gets lonely. He's caretaker for the headquarters of out of state ranch owners, and he still gets up early to watch the sun come up, like he's done since he was a young boy. He still listens for the sound of the coyote or the quail, the bawl of an old cow calling for her calf,—ranch sounds. ....

He watches the sky for signs of a weather change, always hoping that tomorrow will bring the possibility of rain, and feels the contentment of breathing the freshness of the air after the rain finally comes.

Evenings he sits on the front porch and watches night darkening the earth around him as the sun's last glow ebbs from the sky.

What does he know of lonesome? He's surrounded by nature, and mother earth. He's with the things that have always made his life worthwhile. Maybe he can't ride a horse anymore, but he still plays a part in ranch life. He has responsibilities. Driving around in the old ranch pickup, he watches for gates left open, checks on water tanks, directs intruders to the nearest road out of the ranch, and when the absentee owner comes by, it's an unusual visit if he isn't asked for advice on something.

And this old cowboy has his memories, along with the knowledge that he's always done his best and made a "hand," and that will never change. It's called pride, and it's something that's in short supply nowadays, unless you're in cowboy country.

"Haunt his dreams at night"

The title of my book *Time Not Measured by a Clock* is taken from a line in this poem.

What He Left Behind

When the cowboy moved to town,
    he left some things behind,
      but he guessed he'd never need 'em,
        like as not.
The basic tools of his trade,
    gear he'd used every day,
      were sold at auction,
        and some collector bought.

His bridles, bits and saddle,
    his chaps and hackamores,
      all things that through the years
        defined his work,
Were laid out in the ranch yard,
    one cold October day,
      and tagged with numbers
        by the auction clerk.

He didn't stay to watch 'em sell,
    just drove on out the yard,
      as the crowd began to gather
        for the sale.
The ranch had sold that summer;
    this was just the *coup de grace*,
      like a coffin that's received
        the final nail.

He'd cowboyed on this outfit
        for most of thirteen years,
    stayed on once before,
        when the ranch changed hands.
He knew every foot of ground,
        every source of water,
    all the neighbors,
        and all the neighbors' brands.

And he really always thought
        he'd end his workdays here,
    makin' a hand
        as age and health allows.
But the sale this summer
        was to a corporation,
    and their plans included home-sites,
        but no cows.

They asked him to stay on
        and help with inventory,
    and he stayed,
        because he had no place to go.
The job prospects for a cowboy,
        past the age of Medicare,
    are anywhere from none
        to mighty low.

So he put a crew together
    for the final gather,
  tryin' hard to push
    the worry from his mind,
Concentrate on cattle,
    forget about tomorrow,
  when he'd have to leave
    the cowboy life behind.

And then it was finished;
    all the cattle were gone,
  the horses sold;
    his cowboyin' days were through.
He'd found a little place
    way out on the edge of town,
  nothin' fancy,
    but he guessed it'd have to do.

He unpacked the boxes
    that held his belongings,
  and one battered trunk
    containing souvenirs.
This was all that remained
    from a life on the range—
  not much to show
    for workin' fifty years.

On one wall, he hung
       an old Charlie Russell print,
    and a pair of spurs
       inlaid with a silver brand.
And he stood there a while,
       just starin' at the picture,
rememberin' all the years he'd made a hand.

But starting Monday morning,
       he'd be goin' back to work;
    at least it was a way
       to pay the rent.
But bein' on the inside,
       workin' eight to five each day,
    would never keep
       a cowboy's heart content.

All those years spent on horseback,
       "Time Not Measured by a Clock,"
    haunt his dreams at night,
       and replay through his mind,
And though somehow he'll adjust,
       he never will forget,
    the cowboy way,
       and the life he left behind.

Cottonwood Tree

When summer bears down,
      say in August, about noon,
  and the mourning doves tease
      that rain's comin' soon.

But there ain't been a cloud
      in the sky for a week,
  ain't even a puddle
      in the bed of the creek.

141

There's few things, right then,
        that mean more to me,
    than the sight of an old
        green-leafed cottonwood tree.

I was up before dawn
        and I've rode half a day,
    and there ain't been so much
        as a breeze stir my way.

My canteen's almost dry,
        but my shirt's wringin' wet,
    and I *still* haven't found
        all those doggone cows yet!

Then I top one more hill
        and below in a draw,
    is as welcome a sight
        as I ever saw.

A stately old giant
        with a wide canopy,
    where I know there'll be shade
        awaitin' fer me.

And just maybe enough water
        to fill that canteen,
    allow my horse a few swallows;
        he's drawed up and lean.

Wet my neckerchief down,
        to cool my parched face—
    what a pleasure it is
        to find such a place!

'Cause in any cow country,
       where I've ever rode,
    and of all the cowhands
          that I've ever knowed,

You can bet on one thing
       where we *all* agree—
    summer ain't half bad,
          'neath a cottonwood tree!

'Twas The Ride Before Christmas

'Twas the ride before Christmas,
and sure wasn't planned,
   it struck like a bolt from the blue.
He'd saddled his horse
and was gonna check cows,
   which he did everyday, nothin' new.

But he should have untracked
that old cold-backed cayuse,
   'stead, he laid the spurs to his hide,
And like Santa Claus
and his flying reindeer,
   he was off on a pre-Christmas ride.

With a snort and a squeal
his pony reared up,
   then proceeded to buck and pitch.
Whether lettin' off steam,
or bein' plumb mean,
   the cowboy was never sure which.

Each bone-jarrin' jump
tested all of his skill
   at stayin' on top of the saddle,
And it flashed through his mind
he could hurt real bad,
   if that sorry horse won this battle.

But he didn't buck off,
and the horse finally quit,
   confirming what each cowboy knows.
That sometimes the best
Christmas gift he receives,
   doesn't have any wrappin' or bows.

Shortcoming

I never cease to be amazed
    by the things ranch women can do.
Like toppin' off big rank three-year-old colts,
    or tackin' back on a loose shoe.

They pull trailers with their pickup trucks,
    haulin' livestock from place to place.
Back a twenty-foot stock truck up to a chute,
    behind pens where there's dang little space.

And she'd be a poor choice for a burglar,
    who thinks, with no man on the scene,
That he'll just slip in and clean the place out,
    for who'd possibly intervene?

Ha! Who indeed, oh slow-witted fool—
    ya' might as well wake up a bear!
For that helpless woman out there all alone,
    keeps a thirty-eight by her chair!

She's taught a firearms safety class,
    for at least three years in a row.
Rides with the volunteer sheriff's posse,
    and can track an ermine on snow!

A rattlesnake don't stand a chance,
    invadin' her territory,
And neither do coyotes after her hens,
    but that's a whole other story.

These ladies are tough and able,
    and I'm one of the first to praise 'em.
'Cause over the years I've kinda took stock,
    and there ain't much that'll phase 'em.

'Cept for one thing that strikes terror,
    to the heart of the bravest fighter,
And though I ain't never figured out why,
    she's scared to death of a spider!

"Zeb had gotten him close enough to reach the cow"

Boone And Zeb And The Old Cow

Boone and Zeb cowboyed for an Arizona spread that lay south of the Nevada border and north of old Mexico. They'd been partnered for about two years now, and this particular day, contrary to their usual mode of transportation, their horses, they'd filled the old ranch pickup with gas, dumped a load of salt in, and headed out to scatter it—the easy way.

"Ain't this slick?" said Zeb.

"What's that?" answered Boone.

"Not havin' to saddle up, pack a horse with this salt, and ride all day, doin' a job we can do in half a day with this here pickup, and with a lot less energy!"

"Well, maybe," answered Boone, "but I always feel lots better on a horse. When I talk to them, they'll cock an ear, or swish their tail, and I know they're a hearin' me. This pickup don't pay one bit of attention!"

"Ah Boone," said Zeb, "you got to learn to appreciate this modern ranch life more. The younger buckaroos comin' up, why they use pickups a lot. They even say the horse will be ob-so-lete someday!"

"Forget that idea, Zeb." Boone frowned. "There'll never be a replacement for a cowboy's horse, as long as there's any real cowboys left!"

"Well, maybe so, and maybe not," grinned Zeb, "but for my money, this ridin' in comfort, throwin' out salt, is jest fine for a half stove-up old buckaroo!"

Time moved along and the old boys drove mile after mile, scatterin' salt and checkin' the waters, and lookin' for anything might be a problem. And as it happened, that's what they discovered. At one old muddy waterin' hole, bogged down about ten feet from hard ground, was a

149

mossy-horned old cow. She was pretty pathetic lookin', obviously having stood in there quite some time.

"Well, shaw," said Zeb. "That old girl sure enough has herself in a fix!"

"Yea, and from the way she looks," replied Boone, "either we get her out in a hurry, or she's headed for the big range in the sky!"

"How we gonna do that, Boone?" asked Zeb. "We got no horse to pull her out with!"

"Yea," said Boone, "just what I been tellin' ya. But we'll have to make this pickup do. Get my rope out of the truck. Yore gonna drive in close as you can and I'll stand on the front bumper, rope her around those horns, and we'll back up and pull her out."

"Good idea!" nodded Zeb.

Well, Boone took his rope in hand, got on the front bumper of the vintage Dodge and hung onto the ram's head hood ornament, while Zeb put the truck in low gear and eased on down the berm toward the mud at the bottom. The old cow's only movement was one eye that soulfully looked their way.

"O.K." said Boone, "I can almost reach her." He threw, leaning forward precariously, while still hanging on to the front of the truck with one hand, and the rope dropped just short of his target.

"Hang on a minute, Boone," yelled Zeb. "I'll get ya close enough for a good throw!" And with that, he gunned the engine and lurched deeper into the tank.

"No!" hollered Boone, "Don't try to get out any further!" But his warning came too late. Zeb had gotten him close enough to reach the cow, but the wheels of the old truck were now buried in mud up to the hubs. "Well now you've done it!" shouted Boone. "Put it in reverse and see if it'll back up any!"

Zeb put the truck in reverse and revved the motor, but it just settled in further, rear wheels spinning and throwing mud backwards clear out on the bank. "Great," said Boone, "I got the cow caught, but she just died, and you got us stuck deeper than the national debt, out here fifty miles from the ranch!"

"Well, shoot," said Zeb embarrassed like. "I was jest tryin' to help. We've got a chain; maybe we can pull it out."

Boone looked around from his position on the front bumper and said, "We got a ten foot chain Zeb, and there ain't nothin' closer than that tree up there on the top of the bank, and it's a good thirty foot away. 'Course, maybe a tow truck will happen by; or somebody on an elephant!"

By then the sun was getting high in the sky and the morning was heating up. Boone looked at the dead cow at the end of his rope, looked at the tree, then called to Zeb.

"O.K. Make sure you're not in gear, climb out, and take a couple turns around that 'headache rack' with the end of this rope. We're gonna pull this old cow up to the truck."

"She's daid anyway, Boone." said Zeb. "Couldn't that wait 'til later?"

"Don't argue," growled Boone, "just do what I say!"

So Zeb climbed up and looped the rope around the heavy iron rack above the cab. Boone grabbed a hold of the end, and said, "O.K., now together—PULL!"

The old cow was poor, and being dead, there was no resistance, so slowly they managed to get her up out of the mud enough to get her onto her side, and with much sweat and straining, and with Zeb mumbling and grumbling, pulled up to the pickup.

"Now," said Boone, "get out your knife. We're gonna butcher!"

Well, Zeb thought his old partner had indeed lost his marbles, but he knew better than to ask any questions, since Boone already held him responsible for this predicament.

There was no way to accomplish this task other than to get right down in that gooey, smelly mud, so off the truck they got and into the ooze—almost up to their knees.

"Alright," said Boone, "I want her skinned." Zeb looked hard at Boone, looked toward the sky where the sun was starting to bear down, and thought the heat surely had already affected his brain! But skin her they did! Admittedly a rough job, under the circumstances, and when they got done, there wasn't any part below their necks that wasn't covered with mud.

"Now help me pull this hide up in the pickup bed." said Boone, as he stepped up into the truck and began hauling the freshly skinned hide up beside him. Zeb sighed loudly, but grabbed a hold of the other end, and together they got it inside.

"Good," Boone puffed. The day was hot, and both of these two cowhands had passed the half-century mark quite a few years back. "Now," he continued, "we're gonna cut it in one long strip."

Well, Zeb wished he could go for help! His old pard definitely needed to be committed! But Boone sharpened his knife again and began cutting, as Zeb held the hide. By the time this job was accomplished, the sun was at its zenith, and part of the mud and blood was off the cowboys, from the sweat running down their bodies.

"O.K.," said Boone, "tie one end of this strip of hide around the rear bumper." Zeb jumped down and did as requested, while Boone took the rest of the strip, stepped off into the mud, and with his boots making a sucking sound with every step, made his way out of the tank, up to the one lone tree, where he tied the other end securely around the trunk.

"Come on," called Boone, "might as well wait in the shade."

Poor Zeb. "Wait for what?" he pondered. Had Boone thought the old pickup would float out to the middle of the tank and sink? Is that why he tied it to the tree? And was he waiting for *help*? But he grabbed the canteen, wallowed his way through the mud and up on the bank next to his partner.

Boone took a long swig of water, laid back, pulled his hat over his face, and said, "Siesta time, Amigo. You might as well join me. It'll be a while."

"It'll be a while! What'll be a while?" thought Zeb. Oh well, if you can't figure 'em out, join 'em, or somethin' like that! And shrugging his shoulders, he too laid down in the shade, pulled his straw hat over his eyes, and was soon fast asleep. This had been a very strenuous morning, to say the least.

The hours rolled by and Zeb slept soundly, only disturbed by nightmares about a hideless cow that really wasn't dead, but just faking, that got up and was chasing him around and around the tree.

He woke up with a start! What had he heard? Eh-eh-eh creak! Eh-eh-eh creak! Shivers went up his spine despite the fact that it was 115 degrees out in the sun. The old truck, stuck in that muck, was slowly but surely, backing up!

He reached over and quietly shook Boone. "Boone," he called under his breath, "there's somethin' *real* weird goin' on! You better see this!"

Boone sat up, pulled his hat back on his head, smiled, and said, "Yup, there sure is, ain't there? Well, it won't be long now."

Zeb was confounded by what he was witnessing, but he and Boone stood up and watched, as ever so slowly, the old pickup, along with the dehided, dehydrated cow, was pulled and winched backward, until its rear wheels, and then finally the front, were out of the mud and on firm ground once more. It didn't stop there, but once it reached the harder surface it began moving backwards faster. At this point, Boone took his big knife out and deftly cut the piece of rawhide and the truck came to a halt.

"Now Zeb," said Boone, "go get our pickup. We'll drag that carcass out away from here for the coyotes and head back to the ranch. I've had about all I can handle for one day, of your 'half a days job, that takes so much less energy!' This tired old body needs a shower and a cold beer!"

Zeb looked from the now freed pickup with the naked cow still attached, back to the strip of rawhide hanging from the base of the old tree, and shook his head. "How'd ya' *do* that?" he asked.

"Amigo," said Boone, "my daddy was one of the finest rawhide men in the West and I learned early on that green hides will shrink tight as a drum when they dry. So I put two and two together, and it only made sense that as the rawhide dried in this hot sun it would shrink up and pull that darn rig out. But, as I told ya' this mornin', I ain't comfortable doin' on wheels what a good cowboy can do horseback!"

"Ya know," smiled Zeb, "yer right. But I gotta tell ya', for a while there I thought you was crazy! But," he asked as he started for the old pickup, "from now on, would ya' mind if I called ya' Rawhide?"

A Curse On It!

The first time my mother came for a visit,
    I'd been married for over two years.
She'd never spent any time around cowhands,
    so the language was new to her ears.

"When" she asked, "did you start using swear words?
    You were never raised to talk like that!"
"Well Mom," I explained, "some good healthy swear words,
    seem to go with the habitat."

"When you've just been stomped on by a thousand pound horse,
    or run down by some half-crazy cow,
With your wind knocked out, and all bloodied up,
    It's just not enought to say 'ow!'"

"When that green colt you're breakin', dumps you again,
    (that's the second time in a week,)
'Bad horsey! Gee gollies, that really smarts!'
    sure aren't the words that you speak."

"The cows you spend half a day gatherin' are gone,
    'cause somebody left a gate open.
'Well I'll be darned, that's a real shame,'
    are hardly the words that get spoken."

"When you finally get the cattle corraled,
    but no one has shown up with the trucks,
And you see the weight shrinkin' right off their bones,
    it's just not the time for 'Aw shucks!'"

"So turn a deaf ear to my language, Mom,
    it just goes with the territory.
'Cause in the kind of life I'm leadin' now,
    cussin' becomes mandatory!"

155

These next four poems were written by my husband, Dan. He'd never written a poem of any kind, but with some encouragement from me, he put down some stories from his cowboying days, and some from a cowboy's great imagination! The first one, "Long Of Tooth," a term which refers to a horse with a lot of age, was published in *Western Horseman Magazine* way back in 1989. Quite an honor for the first poem he'd ever written.

Long Of Tooth

Dan Jarvis

When I was young and in my prime,
I worked my buns off all the time.

Now that I'm older and I've got more sense,
I don't do windows and I don't do fence.

I'm past the days of ridin' bogs,
So I hang around the corral and train my dogs.

Or ride up in the hills and down the draw.
If I can't do it on a horse, I don't do it at all!

I don't flank calves or pitch no hay,
Just sit on that horse, day after day.

I've got grass to find, and rivers to cross,
There's no one around, so I pretend I'm boss.

I don't fix windmills, or prime no pumps,
I don't dig postholes, or pull out stumps.

I don't plow sod or put up hay,
I just straddle that old pony 'til the end of day.

I don't sleep on the ground with the snakes I dread,
I'm at home at night in my waterbed!

So if some of you punchers still in your prime,
Are scared of bein' caught by old father time,

I'm here to tell you that it's not all bad,
When you turn back the pages and see the fun you had.

And now that I've gotten 'Long of Tooth',
And there's no callin' back the days of my youth,

I've got a degree in wrecks and spills,
So it's good to relax and just ride in the hills.

'Cause I've earned the title of a good buckaroo,
But there's some things left I still want to do.

But I ain't gonna rush, I'll just take my time,
And do 'em all from the back of that old horse of mine.

"*I get me a long stick and start retrievin' my noose*"

Two Old Punchers And The Bear

Dan Jarvis

We got up that mornin'
    before the sun was up,
We'd built a pot of coffee
    and were havin' a cup.
We were sittin' there,
    just sippin' our brew,
Talkin' about things
    we ought to do.

Now me and old Charlie,
    we made a pretty good pair,
Just a couple of old punchers
    with a lot of grey in our hair.
Charlie goes to the stove
    and fills our cups full,
And said, "This would be a good day
    for scattering those bulls.

So we go to the corral,
    and saddle up a couple of hides,
And call for the dogs,
    and start off on our ride.
Now the sun was warm
    and the grass was green,
So we just moseyed along
    and enjoyed the scene.

We talked about things
    we'd like to do,
      We even talked about old times
        when we'd tilted a few.
We talked about this,
    and we talked about that,
      We was just a couple of old cowpunchers,
        chewin' the fat.

We talked about ranges
    where we'd rode,
      We even talked 'bout some
        of the wild oats we'd sowed!
We talked about days
    when we'd ridden hard,
      Now, that old Charlie
        was a pretty good pard!

We ride way up
    under the rim,
      A couple more switchbacks
        and we could see where we'd been.
We graded around
    and came out on the top.
      My old horse planted his feet
        and came to a stop!

I stood up in my stirrups,
      lookin' off to the east,
   A thinkin' that old pony
      might of spotted some beast.
And, sure enough,
      comin' up out of the draw,
   A big brown bear
      was just what I saw.

He came out on the top,
      where the grass was green,
   And no better footing
      had I ever seen.
So I jerked down my rope
      and while buildin' a loop,
   Was a thumpin' that old pony
      with the heels of my boots.

I heard old Charlie say
      as I tore out of there,
   "That crazy ol' bastard's
      gonna rope him a bear!"
Well, the dogs ran in,
      and grabbed the bear by the hide,
   And he slapped old Jake
      way off to the side.

And by that time
    I'm a gettin' there,
  My old lariat's
    just a fannin' the air.
That ol' bear got to thinkin'
    that he'd had enough,
  So he stops his run
    and he calls my bluff.

He stood up on his hind feet,
    just a pawin' the air,
  And I'm tellin' you folks,
    that was one big bear!
So I jerked up my rope
    and give it a spin,
  And it settled 'round his neck
    and just under his chin.

I goes to the horn,
    dallying fast and neat,
  And jerked that old bear
    near off of his feet.
I knew I didn't dare
    give that critter any slack,
  Or he'd be puttin' his footprints
    up the middle of my back.

So I lay my spurs
      to that ol' pony's side,
    And jerk that bear,
       damn near out of his hide!
Then I looked over my shoulder
      and into the sun,
    And Charlie's old pony
      ain't likin' this none!

He's shyin' and snortin'
      and tryin' to rear.
    You'd think that old pony'd
      never seen a brown bear!
But Charlie spins him around,
      and rakes hair from his hide.
    That old Charlie
      could damn sure ride!

I could see his old pony
      beginnin' to slow,
    'Cause Charlie's experience
      was startin' to show.
So I spurred my pony,
      jerkin' that bear,
    'Till he was a bouncin'
      way up in the air.

Charlie sweeps up both hind feet,
    just as sweet as you please,
  And starts his old pony
    to stiffin' his knees.
I'm thinkin' 'bout then
    of turnin' him loose,
  So I get me a long stick
    and start retrievin' my noose.

I told old Charlie,
    "Well, I'm all through,
  Give him some slack
    and let's see what he'll do."
So Charlie rides up,
    and pitches slack in the air,
  And we both put some distance
    between us and that bear.

I told ol' Charlie
    as that bear left on the run,
  "It took me sixty odd years
    to get that job done!"
He said, "Maybe so,
    but I thought we done fair,
  For a couple of old punchers
    with a lot of grey in our hair."

Bear on the rocks—Granite Dells, Prescott, Arizona

"The dogs had 'em held up"

Gatherin' The Remnants

Dan Jarvis

The roundup was over,
    but there was still work to do,
  Pa's tally book tells us
    we're missin' a few.

I'm thinkin' to myself
    I know right where to look,
  'cause ridin' that country's
    like readin' a book.

So I leave the corral
    with a dog named Jake
  and one called
    Bella Blue,

Sittin' straddle
    of a big bay horse,
  that I called
    old Easy Two.

We headed off
    up this big sand wash;
  mesquites,
    they lined the banks,

The dogs were driftin'
    'long behind,
  they never
    broke the ranks.

That old bay horse
     was a movin' out,
  the way
    you like 'em to,

My head was bent down,
     searchin' for sign,
  just like
    I always do.

I picked up the tracks,
     headed up the draw,
   straight towards that thicket
   of old catclaw.

So I swing way around
     to come in from above,
  then I send in the dogs
    to give 'em a shove,

And down in the thicket
     there's a hell of a fuss,
  the brush was a poppin',
    and a big cloud of dust.

The cows were bawlin',
     shakin' the trees,
  so I stepped off my horse
    and get down on my knees.

I'm squatted there peekin'
    in through the brush,
  when out comes the cattle
    in a hell of a rush.

I'm thinkin' 'bout then
    of savin' my hide,
  so I grab for my pony
    and get off to the side.

The cattle come out
    with the dogs on their tail—
  I'm tellin' you all,
    they were packin' the mail!

They went on by,
    lookin' wild and lean,
  but those two old dogs
    stayed right on the scene.

They chased 'em low
    and they chased 'em high,
  it reminded me some
    of wild geese on the fly.

But as for me,
    I needn't worry none,
  because that old bay horse
    could darn sure run.

He ran under a limb
    and ripped off my shirt,
  peeled the bark off my back,
    like I'd been whipped with a quirt.

We dodged a bunch of rocks
    and cactus too,
  and I was wishin' 'bout then
    that I had some glue!

I thought I had things
    about under control,
  'til my horse stuck a foot
    in a badger hole.

So I stepped off,
    way out to the side,
  givin' that pony
    some room to slide.

He slid to a stop
    in a big pile of dirt,
  was a lucky thing
    we didn't get hurt.

I gathered up that wreck
    in a hell of a rush,
  'cause I figured by then
    they'd cleared the brush.

I thought I might of lost 'em,
    to be right frank,
      but the dogs had 'em held up
        by the water tank.

So I sent Jake
    way around,
      to head 'em for the corrals
        they'd never found.

Pa heard us a comin'
    when we graded out of the draw,
      but a big cloud of dust
        was all that he saw.

He started to run
    'cause he knew he had to be fast,
      or those stampedin' cattle
        would already have gone past.

He sets the gates
    and he opens 'em wide,
      and we chased those critters
        right inside.

Pa said,
    "Son, you did right well,
      at gatherin' those remnants,
        but you must have had hell!

From the looks of you
    and your worn out crew,
  it wasn't
    an easy thing to do."

I ride across the corral
    to the other side,
  on that big bay horse
    with the sweaty hide,

And there set
    old Jake and Bella Blue,
  their tongues hangin' out,
    and they were puffin' too.

I stepped off my horse
    and told those three,
  "You all sure saved the day
    for Pa and me."

Now the moral of the story,
    you all know well,
  when you're gatherin' the remnants,
    You gotta ride like hell!

Good cowdogs

"She flipped in the air, did a big hoolihan"

That Bunch-Quittin' Old Heifer

Dan Jarvis

We brought the cows off the mountain
  to the valley below,
'Cause up on the peaks
  it was beginnin' to snow.

We had the cows in the valley
  and were headin' for home,
I was ridin' my favorite,
  that little blue roan.

I rode up to the point,
  lookin' over the herd,
When I spotted that
  bunch-quittin' old heifer,
That could fly like a bird.

She had her nose tipped in the air,
  shakin' her head
  kind of insane,
She'd showed many a puncher
  a lot of that range.

And standin' there
  by that old heifer's side,
Was this long-eared yearlin'
  with no brand on his hide.

You could see that old heifer
    possessed a great need,
Of hidin' that maverick,
    and savin' him for seed!

First she tries for old Barney,
    who's ridin' left flank,
And she damn near outrun him
    to that notch in the bank.

But he turned her around
    and puts her back in the bunch,
But she'll try another puncher;
    I've got me a hunch.

Then she tries for old Willie,
    settin' there on his steed,
And I knew the chances were slim
    of that yearlin' makin' it for seed.

'Cause I knew of old Willie,
    and I knew of his skills,
And the next thing I saw
    was that maverick taking' his spill.

Old Joe turned
    that bunch-quittin' heifer again,
And started headin' her back
    to where her yearlin' had been.

She watched as that maverick
    got up from the ground,
  Still plannin' to hide him
    where he'd never be found.

He got to his feet,
    lookin' awful forlorn,
  His ears were both notched
    and his *huevos* were gone!

So powerful and strong
    is that cow to calf bond,
  All she could think of was takin' him to
    the mountains beyond.

She works her way though the bunch
    headin' my way,
  And the blue roan was ready,
    needless to say.

She left the herd
    with her tail over her back,
  And that little blue roan
    was sure makin' some tracks.

He ran right up,
    by that old heifer's side,
  I had to keep checkin' him,
    or he'd a put tracks on her hide.

I threw down over her right shoulder;
give my wrist a half twist,
I'm a wantin' both front feet,
and I'm not wantin' to miss.

So I goes to the horn
with one thing on my mind,
That was beddin' that old heifer
at the end of my twine.

She flipped in the air,
did a big hoolihan,
Knocked the wind out of her hide,
stuck both horns in the sand.

I let her get to her feet
and then I dumped her again,
And from that day to this,
she's been plumb easy to pen!

Movin' the herd, Wyoming

Jarvis Ranch, Wallowa County, Oregon

When the Time Comes to Leave

For numerous reasons, the time came to move on, to leave the homeplace. Once the uneasy decision was made, the sale was finalized, and we knew where we were going from there, I rather naively thought the hardest part, psychologically, was behind.

But then with the sorting and packing, came other unsettling events. Decisions had to be made as to what would go and what would of necessity be sold, given away, or left behind. At that point it became clear how many memories were tied up in these "things" accumulated through the years. Sometimes the letting go was made more difficult for me, because of the connection to people and times that were no more.

On the last day in that old house, empty rooms echoed as I walked across worn wooded floors, made smooth and a lighter shade by so many thousands of footsteps.

One last time, I peered out through the kitchen window that always whistled when the wind blew, remembering the seemingly endless armloads of firewood we packed into the stove. Marveling how it somehow managed to keep us warm, even in the coldest part of a northwestern winter.

I thought back to all the fences we built, the pastures we irrigated, the cattle we'd run, the good horses we'd ridden, the not-so-good horses we'd ridden, and some we were lucky to get ridden!

Our years there were good, and so are the memories I've kept—even as I left behind a little piece of my heart.

"The cupboards are empty"

Leaving The Homeplace

Tomorrow we leave; it's our last night in this house,
   I've checked, then rechecked, every list.
The cupboards are empty, the dishes all packed,
   I don't see one thing that I've missed.

There's a few bare clothes hangers left in the closet,
   and a little lint on the floor,
But the furniture's gone, except for our bed,
   and we'll sleep in here one night more.

But sleep won't come easy; my mind's wide-awake,
   'though my body is asking for rest.
I've been sorting and packing for weeks now,
   getting ready to empty the nest.

We've spent seventeen years here, our family of four,
   how many sunrises is that?
How many hours of laughter and smiles,
   how much conflict and how much combat?

I can hear the soft sound of the river outside,
   and it helps bring a calm to this night.
One last time, I'll check every room,
   and then I'll turn off the light.

My footsteps sound hollow, the walls seem to stare,
   I'm like a stranger in some other's place.
And all that remains of what used to be,
   are memories, and shadows, and space.

Order Form

❑ Yes! Please send me the following merchandise.

Name_____

Address_____

City_____ State_____ Zip_____

Phone_____Fax_____

Title	Qty.	Each	Total
Time Not Measured By A Clock, Cowboy Poetry by Carole Jarvis	_____	$14.95	_____
	Subtotal		_____
Please add $4.50 for the first item, plus $1.00 for each additional item for shipping and handling.	S&H		_____
Foreign orders must be accompanied by a postal money order in U.S. funds.	TOTAL		_____

Send check or money order to:
Carole Jarvis
43909 W. Hwy. 60
Wickenburg, AZ 85390

To order by phone call (928) 685-2538.
Contact us about discounts.

See our website
www.cowboyshowcase.com